THE INN AT CRYSTAL BAY

MIA KENT

The Inn at Crystal Bay

By Mia Kent

Cover design by Craig Thomas
(coversbycraigthomas@gmail.com)

GET YOUR FREE BOOK!

To instantly receive a free copy of *The Inn at Dolphin Bay*, the first novel in my most popular series, join my Reader Club at www.miakent.com/dolphin.

CHAPTER 1

"This is twisted. This is absolutely twisted."

As Avery Hart half-heartedly squared off against her older sister, she could feel the first tendrils of defensiveness creeping over her, even though she knew Leah was right. More than right, in fact. Of the two of them participating in this conversation, Leah was quite possibly the only sane one.

Still, with a note of defiance she didn't actually feel, Avery shot back, "It's not twisted. It's... perfectly normal." Then, returning her attention to her computer—the screen was blank, but Leah didn't need to know that—she began typing furiously on the keyboard, a highly important message to no one. Her sister watched her with a bemused look, arms crossed, blue eyes narrowed, until finally Avery heaved the loudest sigh she could manage and said, "What? I'm trying to get some work done here, you know."

"And *I'm* trying to talk some sense into you." Leah leaned over the computer and, seeing the blank screen, snorted and shook her head. "Can you please stop pretending to work and actually listen to what I'm saying? I'm worried about you. I don't think that's a crime."

"Of course it's not a crime." Feeling slightly abashed, Avery glanced up from the computer to find her older sister's eyes filled with concern. "But really, what other choice do I have? It's not like I could tell him no."

"You can absolutely tell him no." Leah smacked her palm against Avery's desk for emphasis. "Your ex-husband, the man you're still completely hung up on, wants to marry his fiancée at the inn the two of you bought and restored together. It's bad enough that you're still running the place jointly with him, but a *wedding*? It's torture, Avery. It's going to kill you. Not to mention that it was beyond inappropriate for Danny to even ask that of you in the first place. I know that you're equal partners in this business, but let's face it—the inn is your baby, not his."

"Whoa. Whoa whoa *whoa*." If Avery shook her

head any harder, it would tumble right off her shoulders—not an entirely unwelcome prospect at the moment, given the blessed relief it would provide. "I'm not still 'hung up' on Danny. We work together. We have to get along for the sake of the inn. Period, end of story, that's all, folks. Now if you don't mind, I have to—"

Avery had switched on the computer properly this time, but Leah stopped her with a look that could bring almost anyone to their knees. "I do mind, actually, because I feel like you're not listening to me. You're glossing over everything I'm saying, and... Avery, come on." Leah raked her fingers through her shoulder-length blonde hair in frustration. "Even you have to see that this is madness."

Avery could feel herself crumbling, could feel the hot tears forming behind her eyes, as they so often did whenever the subject of Danny came up. How could they not? The end of their marriage had devastated her, and even though five years had passed since he'd sat her down on the edge of their bed and told her that he loved her, but was no longer *in* love with her, she was still there, in that bedroom, watching as the life she thought was hers broke like glass and shattered at her feet.

She remembered everything about that moment,

a movie reel playing constantly at the edges of her mind, a song of torture that never seemed to end. Danny's brown eyes, full of pity and sorrow and, above all, resolve. The lock of dark hair that fell across his forehead. The hint of smoke in the air, courtesy of a distant beach bonfire. The low murmurs and laughter of her guests in the next room, completely oblivious to her devastation. The numbness that spread over her as his words sank in, starting in her fingertips and spreading all the way to her heart.

She had loved him. She had loved him with everything she had. She had been a good wife, loving and supportive and spontaneous and everything she thought she should be. And he had just... walked away.

"Put yourself in my position, Leah." Avery's voice was imploring as, embarrassed, she roughly swiped away the first tear that dared to trickle down her cheek. "As far as Danny knows, he and I are fine. Molly and I are fine. Which... we are, I guess, all things considered. The Inn at Crystal Bay belongs to Danny just as much as it belongs to me, and if I wanted to get married here"—the thought brought with it a stab of pain, deep in her bones—"he would say yes without hesitation. Why should there be a double standard?"

"Because you weren't the one to end things. You weren't the one to break your vows, and step away from the life you promised to him. You weren't the one to completely rewrite the future."

Leah's voice was rising now, two spots of pink appearing high on her cheeks, and Avery knew that they were no longer just talking about her and Danny. Leah, too, was in the midst of a relationship crisis… if that's what you could call finding out that your husband of twenty-five years had fathered a son with your best friend and kept it a secret for more than a decade.

In the wake of that discovery, Leah had returned home to Crystal Bay, and was currently staying with Avery at the inn while determining her next steps. Even though Leah insisted on a daily basis that she was fine, that she was, in fact, *great*, considering the circumstances, Avery could hear her pacing her room each night, the creaky wooden floorboards a dead giveaway to her sister's insomnia.

How quickly things had changed, for both of them. Unfortunately, Avery knew that the pain of a broken marriage didn't dull with time. At least not for her. Of course, Danny's impending marriage to Molly, who was apparently better than Avery in every way, hadn't helped matters. The knife of betrayal was still there, lodged directly in her heart, twisting deeper every day until she was positive that eventually she would just... keel over.

Danny and Molly probably wouldn't even notice. They'd just step right over her prone body on their way down the aisle, eyes locked on each other, not sparing a thought or concern for anyone else in the world.

With a long, low sigh, Avery sat back in her chair and said, "When did our lives become such a mess?"

At this, the anger on Leah's face melted away, revealing the heartbreak beneath. "I have no idea. Things really are a complete disaster, aren't they?" With a bitter laugh, she said, "At least you have Mom on your side—she's furious at Danny on your behalf. I can't go a single day without her telling me to give Phil another chance. As if *I'm* the one who messed up. When I told her we were separated, she looked horrified. When did she become so invested in my marriage? And more importantly, when did she decide not to take my side?"

Avery merely shook her head. Their mother's behavior was confounding, to say the least, but Cynthia Hart had always been somewhat of an enigma, the polar opposite of her daughters. Then, glancing out the inn's picture window to see a pair of cars pulling into the parking lot, Avery straightened up and said, "They're here," not bothering to hide the anxiety in her voice. Turning to Leah, she shooed her away with the words, "Make yourself scarce. The last thing I need right now is you standing in the corner and glowering at everybody."

"But glowering is my specialty," Leah protested, her lips curving up in the barest hint of a smile before she turned and headed for the staircase, stopping with one hand on the banister. "Fine, I'll go. But if you need backup, you know where to find me." Then she was gone, leaving Avery to hastily check her reflection in her compact mirror and pat her dark hair into place just as the car doors opened and the passengers began to step out.

Her desk phone chose that moment to come to life, the two short rings indicating that the call was coming from one of her guest rooms... and Avery didn't have to wonder who might be on the other end of the line. Max Wallace, her newest check-in who had arrived only that morning, was already proving to be the most difficult guest she'd had all year. The first call had come a mere two minutes after he'd entered his room, complaining to her that the temperature was two degrees too high—he

7

preferred a comfortable sixty-eight, thank you very much. That was followed in short order by the bathroom soap irritating his sinuses, the writing desk he'd specifically requested—an old wooden desk she'd unearthed from storage and lugged down to the room herself—being too small, and the curtains letting in too much light.

By the fourth complaint, she was grinding her teeth, her voice saturated with politeness as she assured him over the phone that she would handle the latest "problem." Of course, she would *like* to handle it by packing his bags for him and marching him toward the front door. But for reasons unknown to Avery, Max had booked a two-month stay at the inn, and with business generally being slow in Crystal Bay, a tiny town along Florida's Forgotten Coast, she could scarcely afford to turn away paying customers, irritating though they might be.

Choosing just this once to let the voicemail pick up, Avery rose from her chair just as the inn's front door opened and Danny bounded in, eyes shining with excitement, smile wide as his gaze landed on her. "Avery! Just the woman we've been dying to see."

He gestured at the three women crowding into the foyer behind him, two of whom she recognized right away. "You already know Molly and my mom, of course," Danny said before turning to the third woman, who was studying Avery with unmistakable interest. "And this is Susan, Molly's mother. Susan, this is Avery, my good friend and co-owner of The Inn at Crystal Bay."

Avery's cheeks heated at his use of the word "friend," and she winced automatically—but quickly did her best to cover it up with a polite smile. "Susan, it's lovely to meet you. I'm glad you could make it to our little tour today. Not that these two need it," she said, nudging Danny in the arm in an attempt at playfulness that was cringeworthy at best. "Danny knows every square inch of this place, probably better than I do!"

Molly laughed appreciatively, tucking her arm into Danny's as the diamond engagement ring he had recently slipped on her finger sparkled almost obscenely in the rays of sunlight streaming in through the window. "True, but we thought it would be fun to have a tour anyway, see it from a different perspective, get a sense of what it might look like on the big day. Danny tells me you've never held a wedding here before, which is a shame, since it's such a stunning place. What a missed opportunity!"

"What can I say, we've had our hands full just

running the inn, let alone trying to plan events here too." Danny patted Molly's hand lovingly, his smile turning more adoring by the second—and Avery's breakfast churning more aggressively in her stomach to match it. "But if we ever decide to go down that road, then I think it's only fitting for you and me to hold the inn's inaugural ceremony and reception, don't you agree?"

No. No no no no *no*.

That wasn't fitting. In fact, Avery thought, manic grin now stretched tightly across her face, that was the exact *opposite* of fitting.

What would have been fitting? Avery and Danny renewing their vows here, in the place they had built together, the place they had stored their hopes and dreams for the future. The two of them listening to their children scampering through the inn's hall-ways, or watching them splash in the ocean waves mere steps from the inn's front door. What would have been fitting was late nights on the porch swing, snuggled up together and watching the stars blanket the midnight sky, or waking up to an apricot sunrise that took their breath away.

What would have been fitting was anything, *anything*, but this.

Susan's expression had turned sympathetic, as if

she was the only one who could read Avery's thoughts. "You know, I just remembered I have an important call to make for work in a little while," she said, checking her watch. "Why don't we get on with the tour, then?" Her eyes met Avery's once more, and Avery did her best to convey a look of gratitude before focusing her full attention on the newly engaged couple.

"I've been giving it some thought," she said, "and I've come up with two spots I think would be perfect for the ceremony—one by the gazebo in the side yard, and one right on the sand in front of the inn. Why don't we check out the gazebo first?"

Then, heart in her throat, knot in her stomach, tears in her eyes, she turned and led the love of her life—and the love of *his* life—out into the blazing Florida sunshine.

"Good afternoon, Ms. Turner, this is Harrison Parker with Parker & Sons Law Group. My secretary forwarded me your request for an attorney to represent you in your divorce filing, and I would be happy to oblige. Please give me a call when you have an opportunity and we can work out—"

Leah ended the voicemail with a punch of her finger against her cell phone and a ball of dread in her stomach. It was hard to believe that twenty-five years of marriage, and several years of dating before then, not to mention two children, a house in the suburbs, and what she thought was a happy life, had culminated in... this. A call from a divorce attorney. A call she never would have imagined receiving.

They had been so happy, the two of them, for so many years. Despite watching plenty of friends and acquaintances weather rocky marriages and, ultimately, separation and divorce, she had always been secure—smug, even—in the knowledge that she and Phil were safe. Rock-solid. Above all of that nonsense. They were the golden couple, at least in her own head.

Who could have guessed that one secret, one hideous, life-altering secret, could bring them to their knees?

Not her. Not ever.

But here they were all the same. Leah couldn't shake the sound of the attorney's voice, couldn't erase his use of "Ms." instead of "Mrs.", a title she'd held proudly for the better part of a lifetime. She dropped her cell phone on the bed and then walked over to the window, gazing out at the turquoise sea that stretched before her, the stunning white-sand beaches beckoning to anyone who passed, the cloudless sky dotted here and there with seagulls swooping in and out of the sunshine.

She heard the distant sound of the inn's front door closing, then watched as Avery, shoulders hunched, led a small group of people toward the gazebo, Danny and Molly among them. Leah's heart ached for her sister, but she turned away from the scene—it was too much for her right now, when she was at the lowest point in her life. Instead she watched a mother and her young son playing in the sand nearby, pails and shovels at their feet, colorful beach umbrella rippling in the gentle breeze. They looked so happy, so carefree, their shoulders brown from the sun, their hair tangled with saltwater. She would have given anything to join them. To be them.

Her cell phone rang, nearly causing her to jump out of her skin, and Leah turned from the window to glance at the caller ID, a knot of apprehension working its way up her throat. Phil had been calling too much these days, trying to persuade her to come home, to try therapy again, to work things out, to give them a *chance*, in his words, as though he deserved one. Most of the time he was near tears or openly weeping, whispering words of regret and heartbreak that did little to thaw the coldness that had settled over her whenever she thought of him.

And Kate. And what they had done.

Sleeping with another woman was one thing. But sleeping with your wife's best friend? Fathering a secret child with her?

That was a level of betrayal Leah never would have imagined Phil was capable of.

With a wave of relief, she saw that it wasn't Phil calling her but Callie, her youngest child and only daughter. They hadn't spoken much in the past few days since Leah had broken the news to her two children that their parents' marriage was over, just a few text messages she'd sent that largely went unanswered. She didn't push Callie to respond, knowing that her daughter needed time to process an abrupt end to what she had always viewed as a stable, happy, fairy-tale relationship. Not to mention that Callie had always been a daddy's girl, the apple of her father's eye; he was her first choice of parent since she was old enough to open her eyes and latch on to Phil's adoring ones.

Andrew, on the other hand, had been in touch with Leah at least once a day to check up on her, see if she needed anything, make sure she was all right. He had been a sensitive boy since childhood, the first to pick up on other people's emotions, to slip his hand into theirs if he sensed they needed it. And right now, she needed it. Desperately. He lived five hours away, but whenever he reached out to her, she felt as though he were beside her, wrapping her in one of his famous bear hugs guaranteed to melt her troubles away.

Feeling slightly apprehensive at the thought of speaking to her daughter, Leah answered the phone with a cautious, "Hello?" Then she waited, holding her breath, wondering how much damage the implosion of her and Phil's marriage was going to cause her relationship with Callie. And how much had already been done.

"Mom, hi!" Callie's voice was sunny, breezy, completely at odds with what Leah had expected. She felt her breathing return to normal as she clutched the phone in one hand like a lifeline, the relief washing over her in waves. The last time they spoke, Callie had barely returned one-word answers, and when she did, each syllable was filled with bitterness and blame. Leah had done her best to take it in stride; after all, she'd chosen not to fill her daughter in on the gruesome details of Phil's betrayal, and in Callie's mind, Leah was the one who had gone off the deep end by walking away from twenty-five years of wedded bliss.

"Hi, honey, how are you? I'm so glad to hear from you." As she spoke, Leah glanced out the window, her eyes trailing to the horizon, where a row of sailboats bobbed in the gentle wind, their sails fluttering and gleaming in the brilliant Florida sunshine. Dealing with the heartbreak of a failed marriage was slightly easier, she decided, when you could lick your wounds in paradise.

"I'm great. Listen, I'm calling because I wanted to see if you were available to grab dinner this weekend. Saturday night?" Leah could hear voices in the background, followed by the clink of mugs, and knew that Callie was sitting in her favorite coffee shop on campus, the place where the two of them had met up on countless occasions over the past few years to catch up, precious mother-daughter time that meant the world to her.

"I'd love to have dinner with you." Leah's answer came quickly, eagerly, her heart lightening at the olive branch her daughter was dangling in front of her. "What's the occasion?"

"Jeremy." Callie's voice softened on the name. "I know we've only been dating for a few weeks, but we've known each other forever, and I think things are starting to get serious. I wanted all of you to meet him, start getting to know him. In case..." She trailed off, leaving the remainder of the sentence unfinished, but her happiness and excitement were palpable, even over the phone.

Leah barely registered any of that, though. Instead, she froze in place, heart suddenly jack-hammering against her ribcage. "All of us? As in..."

"You and Daddy, of course, and I even managed to convince Andrew to take some time off work and join us." Callie hesitated. "That won't be a problem, will it?" The words came out as an accusation, and Leah flinched. She knew she couldn't avoid Phil forever, of course, knew that he would always be an important part of family functions and special cele-brations... but the thought of seeing him again now was an open wound, raw and bleeding. In that moment, Leah couldn't imagine anything worse than doing something as mundane as sharing a meal with him.

"Of course it's not a problem. It's not a problem at all." The fake cheerfulness Leah injected into her tone was enough to cause a ball of nausea to settle at the base of her throat. She imagined the scene: her family sitting at a restaurant, like they'd done count-less times over the years, laughing and talking and pretending that everything was okay when it absolutely wasn't.

And never would be again.

Because as much as she wanted to arrive at a place of peace with Phil, she knew that was a goal for the distant future, when her heart had healed and the simple act of sitting across from him didn't fill her with a terror so pure she actually felt like it was strangling her.

But this wasn't about her. Nor was it about Phil. This was about Callie, and Leah refused to let the current crisis in her marriage come between them. She wouldn't let Phil ruin one more important relationship in her life. She'd already lost her husband and her best friend. She would fight tooth and nail to keep her daughter, no matter how much it killed her.

And so it was with a newfound determination that Leah added, "You name the place and time, and I'll be there." Callie couldn't see that she was white-knuckling the phone, or had sunk onto the bed, knees trembling, or that she felt like all the air had been sucked out of the room at once. Her daughter only knew that Leah was her rock, her safe place, and nothing would ever change that.

"Awesome." She could practically hear Callie

grinning over the phone, could envision how her blue eyes, so like Phil's, were lighting up with excitement. "I know you're going to love him. I'll text you the details later, okay? Gotta run, class in a few minutes." She hung up with barely a goodbye, leaving a still-frozen Leah to stare blankly at the phone, wondering what in the world she had just agreed to.

CHAPTER 2

*B*enjamin Grant withdrew the battered silver key from his pocket and slipped it into the lock, the act as familiar to him as breathing. The scuffed wooden door stuck, as it always did, and probably always would, but a nudge with his shoulder in just the right spot jolted it into submission, and it swung open to reveal the dim, slightly damp interior of the place where Ben had spent the better part of a lifetime.

His grandfather had opened The Beach Bum nearly seventy years ago, and it had quickly developed a reputation as the best dive bar along this quiet stretch of Florida's Forgotten Coast. Always filled with the low chatter and laughter of residents and tourists alike, it had become a second home to

Ben once his father had taken over the daily operations, and fifteen years ago, the torch had been passed to him. There was never a question what Ben was going to do with his life; the bar was in his blood, in his bones, just as much as the sand and sea and sun.

As he stepped inside, he inhaled deeply, taking in the familiar scent of musty carpeting and damp walls that he loved so much. This was a beach bar through and through, a place where his patrons could kick off their shoes—literally—and escape the stressors of life for a while, all in the most beautiful setting Ben had ever seen.

In his youth, he'd had the opportunity to travel the world, and he'd stood in the shadows of magnificent architecture, walked cobblestone streets that dated back centuries, gazed out at the most famous natural wonders of this great planet... but never once had any of them compared to Crystal Bay, his home, the place his soul yearned for. To Ben, there was nothing more breathtaking than watching a grapefruit sunrise over the glistening turquoise water, or sinking his toes into the white sand that sparkled like glass for miles in all directions. There was nothing more fulfilling than living in a town where everyone knew you, and more importantly, where they cared about you.

He'd never understood the allure of living in a big city, where no one knew you, where no one cared where you had been or where you were going. Where your story, unique and precious that it was, simply didn't matter. He'd never understood how Leah could just walk away from everything she'd once held so dear.

But now she was back, he reminded himself as he flipped on the lights and moved toward the bar to begin preparing the usual drinks for his afternoon regulars, who would start trickling in over the next few minutes. Now she was back, and they could begin making up for the years, the *decades*, they had lost. So much time. So much wasted time.

The bar door creaked open and Ben glanced up, hand already raised in a silent greeting to Chet, his father's best friend and the first to stop in most days, often just to sit and chat with Ben for a while on his way home from the fishing trawler he worked on. After Ben's father passed away a decade ago, Chet had stepped in to fill his shoes the best he could, an honorary role neither of them took lightly. Anytime he needed advice, or an ear to listen, Chet was there, day or night, family in every way that mattered.

"How's it going, boyo?" Chet asked, face ruddy from saltwater and sun, gray hair tousled from the wind. His hands were rough and calloused, a testament to the decades he'd spent out on the open water, and his skin was several shades darker than his natural complexion, even in the winter.

Sliding onto the bar stool across from Ben, he accepted the glass of ginger ale Ben slid his way and tossed a handful of peanuts into his mouth. The first handful was quickly followed by a second, then a third, until Ben, eyebrows raised, grabbed the jumbo-sized container he kept behind the bar and refilled the bowl.

"Hungry, are we?" he asked as Chet eyed the bowl for a fourth round before apparently thinking better of it and focusing on his ginger ale instead. That, too, was gone in a flash, the glass sliding back toward Ben for a refill.

"Hot day." Chet removed his ubiquitous ballcap and wiped the sweat from his weathered brow. "Don't know how many more years of this I have left in me."

Ben smiled at the familiar words; Chet had been threatening to retire for at least twenty years now, but the call of the sea was too much for him, a siren always drawing him back in with her seductive song. "When you finally decide to hang up your net, you can join me here. I could use another pair of hands."

Chet snorted. "Especially when you're up on that stage with your guitar. Heard you brought down the house again last night." He pulled the peanut bowl toward himself, began sorting through it with one finger. "I keep meaning to stop by one of these evenings to hear you play, but Doreen and I are tucked up in bed by nine. Need my beauty sleep, and Lord knows she needs hers."

Ben laughed. Anyone who didn't know better would think that Chet had just insulted his wife, but the man was a lifelong bachelor. Doreen was his ancient English bulldog, with a comical underbite and a face so wrinkled only Chet himself could love it.

"I shudder to think what would happen if she didn't get it," he replied, elbows propped on the counter as he gazed up at the makeshift stage his bartender Kody had set up for when Ben brought out his guitar. The first time had been on the losing end of a bet, but every night since, he'd fielded enough requests from his regulars that he decided to make it a semi-regular thing. And despite the usual on-stage jitters, he found that he still loved playing—

something he hadn't done much in the years since Leah had left.

Not that he hadn't tried. He had, more times than he could count. But the day she drove away, she'd taken his heart... and his music.

"I hear she's back." Chet had stopped flicking through the peanuts and settled his full attention on Ben, face serious, as though reading the younger man's mind. "Leah Hart."

"Leah Turner now." Ben nodded, keeping his voice nonchalant. "And yes, she's back in town. She's staying at her sister's inn for a while."

"So I heard." Chet studied his glass of ginger ale, tracing his finger along the beads of condensation that had formed before taking a healthy sip. "Remi told me." His faded green eyes swept over Ben's face in a way he found unnerving. "She isn't too happy about the news, I'll tell you that. Wants me to talk some sense into you."

Ben frowned. "Talk some sense into me about what? I didn't have anything to do with Leah coming back to Crystal Bay. She and Phil were having marital problems."

Chet grunted. "And you didn't suggest she come home for a while? Your sister seems to think you had a hand in it."

"I had a hand in nothing." Ben raked his fingers through his dark hair in frustration that Chet and his sister were discussing him behind his back. "Leah was upset, she confided in me over the phone, and I told her if she needed to get away for a while, clear her head a little bit, she might consider coming home." He shrugged. "It's what any friend would say."

"You're not any friend." Chet chuckled, then held up his hands. "Hey now, I'm not saying you did anything wrong. I'm just telling you that Remi is worried about you. She's afraid you're going to have your heart broken again." He fell silent, his eyes studying Ben's face again. "She's still a married woman, you know. There's every chance she and her husband might work things out."

The words were an arrow aimed directly at Ben's heart. Ignoring the stab of pain, he made another attempt at nonchalance by raising one shoulder in a casual shrug. "That's none of my business. And as for getting my heart broken again…" He gazed out the window toward the sea, rippling gently and glittering in the blazing afternoon sunshine. "I have no expectations."

The lie was a tangible thing, and Ben could feel it twisting and writhing in the air around them before settling on his chest, a weight that had been constricting his breathing day and night, ever since she walked back into his life and seemed poised to stay.

Chet was silent for several long moments after that. Then, "I see." He stretched, then rose from the table. "Like I said, I'm just passing on a message. You're a grown man, and you can figure things out for yourself." He rapped his knuckles on the counter once. "But don't be too mad at Remi. She's not trying to meddle, she just cares about her big brother."

He finished the last of his drink, then nodded at Ben. "You need me, you know where to find me. I better get home before Doreen wakes up. She pines after me, you know. If she can't find me, her howls will disturb the whole neighborhood."

He was almost to the door when it opened again and, stepping aside, he nodded to Leah, who entered the bar and made a beeline for Ben. Her eyes were red-rimmed, her face was splotchy, her hair was tangled... and she had never looked more beautiful. Ben swallowed hard and caught Chet's eye; the older man gave him a knowing nod before stepping out into the sunshine, ballcap in hand, whistling a tuneless melody under his breath, the sound echoing around the bar long after the door swung closed behind him.

Ben turned to Leah, who had collapsed onto the same bar stool Chet had just vacated. She was slumped over the counter, running her hands through her hair, face a mask of despair. Ben's heart sank; he knew all too well what the topic of conversation would be, and should be, given that Leah was going through the lowest point in her life. And even though Ben was happy to offer her a shoulder to cry on as she navigated the end of her marriage, he found the constant discussions about Phil draining, and exhausting, an unbearable reminder that she had ultimately chosen him over her home, over Crystal Bay... over Ben.

"You won't believe the day I've had." Leah grabbed a paper napkin from a nearby stack and blotted her eyes, then dabbed at her nose. "First I heard from the divorce lawyer, and he's more than willing to represent me." She presented the news as if it were a negative, and Ben wrinkled his forehead in confusion.

"That's... bad?" he asked, trying to keep the genuine bewilderment out of his tone. He filled a glass with ice water and passed it to her; she accepted it with a grateful smile.

29

"No, it's good. I guess?" She sighed, long and loud, and shook her head, blonde hair swinging over her shoulders. "But after twenty-five years of marriage, it's not exactly a call I wanted to be making. Hearing that lawyer's voice, hearing him say the word 'divorce,' it just makes it all sound so... real. And surreal." Leah gazed vacantly into her water glass. "I can't believe it's actually happening. When I married Phil, I truly believed it was forever."

"Are you having second thoughts?" The question came out sharper than Ben had intended, but Leah didn't seem to notice. Heart in his throat, he waited for her to shake her head... which she did, eventually, though the gesture seemed half-hearted.

"No, of course not. But that doesn't make any of this less painful. I'm furious at Phil, but that doesn't wipe out the last three decades. It's just... hard to come to terms with, is all."

Ben breathed a covert sigh of relief. Hard to come to terms with—that, he could deal with. It made perfect sense. But if Leah changed her mind, if she decided to reconcile with Phil, if he lost her again, this time permanently...

No. Do not go there.

"And then Callie called." Leah's eyes welled up with tears. "She wants the whole family to go out to dinner this weekend to meet her boyfriend." She gave Ben a desperate look. "How am I supposed to do that? How am I supposed to sit there and play nice? This whole thing is a nightmare. I didn't ask for it, and I want no part in it, but I can't seem to escape it. Is this what life is like now? Trying to avoid Phil? Not wanting to celebrate with my own children? It makes me sick." She pushed the water glass away and settled her eyes on Ben... those beautiful blue eyes he'd been getting lost in for as long as he could remember.

He took a deep breath, allowing himself a few moments before responding. Right now, he needed to don his "friend" cap, not wave his "I'm in love with Leah" banner, as he so desperately wanted to. She knew that he had feelings for her, though she had no inkling just how deep they ran—how deep they had always run. She knew, ultimately, what he wanted. The ball was squarely in her court, but Ben was all too aware that she needed time to sort through her own feelings. Rushing into a relationship was the worst thing they could do, because Ben was no rebound. He was her soulmate—he just needed her to recognize that.

Finally, he settled on, "Things won't always be so bad. This is new... for everyone."

"I know." Leah raised her head, meeting his eyes for the first time. A look of understanding passed between them, and she cringed. "I'm sorry. I'm sure this is the last thing you want to be talking about." She dabbed at her eyes again as a fresh wave of tears threatened to form. "I'm just so lost right now, Ben. I'm a mess."

She fell silent for a moment, and when their eyes met again, the barest hint of a smile was playing around her lips. "If you can believe it, I didn't actually come here to complain to you about Phil and the disaster my life has become. You've heard plenty of that recently. I came here to ask you if you wanted to grab lunch with me tomorrow. Just... as friends. Right now."

The disappointment hit him hard, but he took great pains not to show it. Instead, with a casual smile that matched her own, he said, "Sounds great. Picnic on the beach?"

Leah laughed. "You know me too well." Then, smoothing down her hair, she stood from the stool and said, "I have to get back to the inn—I promised Avery I'd help her prepare a couple of the guest rooms for tomorrow's check-ins. I'll see you soon, okay?" She hesitated a moment, then added, "And Ben? Thanks... for listening, for being there, for everything you've done over the past couple of weeks. I don't know what I'd do without you."

"No problem." Ben waved an airy hand, the relaxed gesture completely at odds with the elephant-sized weight still settled on his chest. "You know you can always talk to me."

She gave him a grateful smile and turned to leave, tossing him one last look over her shoulder before pushing open the door and stepping outside.

"I don't know what I'd do without you either," he murmured to the door as it closed with a soft *thunk*. Because now that she was back in his life, he intended to keep her there.

He intended to show her that it should have been him all along.

AVERY SLIPPED BEHIND her desk with a sigh, determined to keep her eyes on her computer, and not on Danny saying a thoroughly nonverbal goodbye to Molly in the inn's parking lot. The past few hours had been the most draining she'd experienced since the day she signed the divorce papers, with her an unwilling participant as her ex-husband and his bride-to-be practically skipped through the inn like

a couple of kids, pointing out all the perfect loca-
tions for the perfect wedding that the perfect couple
was planning.

She was not bitter. She was not... anything.
Sometime in the second hour of wedding-planning
bliss, an emptiness had settled over her, as though
she were watching the events from a distance, the
armor she'd donned so thick it was practically
impenetrable.

Practically. It hadn't kept the tears from blurring
her vision when the happy couple acted out their
vows right there on the sand, complete with a
passionate kiss that sealed the deal... and Avery's
fate.

"Not yet," she murmured to herself, eyes drifting
to the window despite her best efforts. "They aren't
married yet."

That meant there was still a chance he would
reconsider. There was still a chance he would realize
that the day he gave Avery up was the day he lost his
mind. Of course, she'd been waiting for that to
happen for five years now, and every day that passed
slimmed the chances that he would ever understand
just what he had lost. What *they* had lost.

In a word? Everything.

I'm so sorry, Avery. I love you—you know I do. But

I'm just not in love with you anymore, and we both deserve better.

She shook her head to banish the words, as clear to her now as the day he whispered them to her, tears in his eyes, his grip on her hand tremulous. Outside the window, Danny was giving Molly one last hug before helping her into the car, then he was bounding across the parking lot and up the porch steps to the front door, bursting through it before Avery could arrange her face into a neutral expression. She did so quickly, assuming a businesslike appearance that screamed indifference as she typed on the keyboard, looking up the week's reservations that she already knew by heart.

"That was really something, wasn't it?" Danny leaned across the desk and planted a chaste kiss on the top of Avery's head, leaving a burning imprint where lips met skin. "Have I ever told you that you're the best?"

"Not nearly enough." Avery gave him a cheerful smile that masked her rapidly beating heart. She gazed up at him, fingers curling on the keyboard to prevent them from wandering to his face, his stubble, the adorable dimple in his chin that she had spent years staring at. It was no longer hers to touch.

"Well, you are." Danny leaned against the desk

then, arms crossed, looking thoughtful. "You know, after seeing the inn with fresh eyes and hearing what Molly had to say... I think she's on to something. With the inn, the scenery. It's all so beautiful, you know?" He waved his arm toward the window, toward the sea beyond. "We should be holding weddings here, maybe other events too. It could add a significant amount of revenue."

"And a significant amount of work," Avery pointed out. "The two of us already have our hands full just running the day-to-day operations. Adding events into the mix? We'd never get a wink of sleep."

"Sure we would, once Molly joins us full time."

He threw the statement out casually, as if they had discussed it. As if she had agreed to such a thing. Avery could feel a numbness spreading through her limbs, a growing sense of disbelief. It was bad enough that Molly had steadily encroached on her territory since she and Danny had grown serious, but this? A full-time job at the inn? Facing the two of them all day, every day?

It was unthinkable. It was heartless. It was a terrible, foolish, cruel idea.

"Molly's planning on working here full time?" Avery was careful to keep a neutral tone, careful to keep up the façade of pleasant, happy, agreeable ex-wife. Always agreeable. "I didn't realize the two of you had discussed that."

"Well, it's only natural." Danny picked up a pen from the desk and began twirling it idly between his fingers. "Her job at the bank isn't the most exciting, and she's loved the time she's spent working at the inn. She's found her passion here, and besides, we could really use the help." He gave Avery a roguish wink. "She's even willing to clean toilets."

"Isn't she a saint." Avery's smile was now stretched so wide her cheeks ached. "But Danny... I'm not sure we can afford another staff member. You and I aren't exactly rolling in dough, you know." Between the inn's upkeep and day-to-day expenses, Avery and Danny both took home a small but comfortable paycheck twice a month. Adding a third employee would stretch their finite resources to the max.

"Oh, don't worry about that." Danny waved his hand again, the picture of nonchalance. "I'm sure she'd be fine taking a small salary to start, and if she starts bringing in business with weddings and other events, she'll more than pay for herself."

At this, Avery fell silent. What more was there to say? Danny had thought of everything—and so too, apparently, had Molly. Only she was left in the dark, yet again.

This is twisted. This is absolutely twisted.

Leah's words chose that moment to invade Avery's brain. She banished them with a shake of her head—*hard*—that had Danny eyeing her in concern.

"Everything okay?" he asked, squinting in her direction.

"Just a mosquito." Avery took a deep, slow, steadying breath, then turned her attention back to the computer. "If you don't mind, I need a few minutes to go through these reservations. I'll catch up with you later, okay?"

"Okey-dokey." Danny pushed off from the counter with his trademark happy-go-lucky grin, not noticing, never noticing, Avery's abrupt change in demeanor. Only when he had rounded the corner and disappeared from view did Avery let out the breath she was holding and turn her gaze toward the window, staring vacantly at the picturesque ocean scenery while imagining how it would feel to spend each day pretending she and Molly were pals.

This inn was hers. It was *hers*, and slowly but surely, it was being taken away from her, an erosion she felt powerless to stop.

"You look like someone stole your kitten."

Avery jumped at the sound of Leah's voice; she hadn't heard her sister come in. Smoothing down her hair, she graced Leah with what she hoped resembled a genuine smile and said, "Just lost in thought, nothing important." Eyeing her sister, she added, "Where did you run off to?"

"The Beach Bum." Leah dropped into the seashell-patterned armchair in the foyer and leaned her head against the cushion with a sigh. "I went to ask Ben if he wanted to have lunch with me tomorrow, but instead I ended up spilling my guts about Phil. Again." She tucked a strand of blonde hair behind her ear and shook her head. "I'm sure he loves that, given… everything."

"You mean given the fact that he's in love with you and desperately wants you for himself." Avery gave her sister a pointed look. "Yes, I can see how that would be a problem for him."

"He's not in love with me." Leah laughed softly. "He's just…"

"In love with you." Avery cocked her head and regarded her older sister with amusement. "He's just waiting for you to open your eyes and see that you feel the same way about him, and have since you were a kid."

"That's not fair," Leah protested, eyes sparking

with annoyance. "That would make it seem as if my marriage to Phil wasn't genuine, and that's the furthest thing from the truth. Yes, it's true that I had feelings for Ben way back when, and I'm open to the idea of exploring things with him once the dust has settled with Phil and the divorce and the kids... but in the years since I left Crystal Bay, he and I have maintained a friendship, and nothing more."

"Okay, okay." Avery held up her hands in a playful attempt to ward off her sister's anger. "I'm just trying to point out the obvious; don't shoot the messenger."

Then, just as Leah leaned forward in her chair, opening her mouth hotly to respond, the sound of footsteps descending the inn's creaky staircase reached their ears. A few moments later Max Wallace appeared in the foyer, and Avery had to stifle a groan when she took in his expression— annoyed, the same way he looked every time she'd seen him over the past six hours.

"Mr. Wallace!" Her voice couldn't have been any more sickeningly sweet if she'd doused herself in syrup. "How can I help you?"

She folded her hands on the desk and gave him a patient, expectant look, though inwardly she could feel the steam rising. The inn wasn't perfect, of course, but the vast majority of her guests were charmed by the old Victorian house that she and Danny had painstakingly restored and filled with loving touches. Not this man, though. He was either used to five-star accommodations... or was just a plain old pain in the behind.

"The walls are too thin," he spat, bracing his hands against the desk and glaring down at Avery. "I can hear... *everything*... going on in the room next to mine." He gave her a disgusted look. "If I wanted a show, I'm sure I could find something suitable on the Internet."

Beside her, Leah was stifling a snort of laughter behind her hands, and Avery had to work hard to keep a straight face as she squared off with the furious Max. "I'm so sorry, sir," she said, voice still dripping with honey. "I could offer you a pair of earplugs... or I could personally knock down your wall and stuff in some more insulation. Whichever you'd prefer."

The words were out of her mouth before she could stop them—he was just so darn *infuriating*—and by now, Leah's shoulders were shaking with suppressed laughter.

"That won't be necessary." Two bright spots of color appeared on Max's cheeks, and for a moment,

MIA KENT

he actually looked embarrassed. But it was there and gone in a flash, replaced by a coolness in his eyes that let Avery know in no uncertain terms that he hadn't appreciated the sarcasm.

He opened his mouth to say more, then closed it again before turning and practically stomping out of the foyer. His footsteps pounded back up the staircase, and a minute later, they heard the distant *thud* of his door slamming.

"Well that was unprofessional of me." Avery winced, annoyed with herself for her lack of hospitality. Max Wallace may have been a nuisance, but he was still a guest, which meant that she had a responsibility to listen to his concerns and address them the best she could. That whole business with Danny and Molly must have been getting to her more than she realized—she needed to rein in her emotions, stat.

"I'm just amazed my sweet, shy Avery is speaking that way to a VIP," Leah chimed in, a knowing smirk on her face. "You *do* know who that is, don't you?"

Avery gave her sister a blank look. "I have no idea what you're talking about. His name is Max Wallace —that's as much information as I have about him."

"Oh, my dear sister, have you been living under a rock?" Leah sighed and shook her head playfully.

42

"His name isn't just Max Wallace—he's *the* Max Wallace." When Avery continued staring at her in confusion, she said, "The famous author? The one whose wife is a big-time Manhattan socialite? She's even on one of those reality television shows about the lives of rich and famous women. Callie and I used to watch it all the time."

Avery shrugged. "Sorry, no idea what you're talking about. But I'll take your word for it that he's 'very important.' A very important thorn in my side. At this point, I don't care if he's the king of England. I just want him to stop complaining to me about everything."

"He's handsome," Leah continued, as if Avery hadn't even spoken. "Don't you think? Those ocean-blue eyes, the salt-and-pepper hair... he may be a pain, but he's definitely easy on the eyes."

"I hadn't noticed." Avery's voice was curt, because in truth, she hadn't. She didn't notice most men these days—she only had eyes for the one she couldn't have.

And Max Wallace couldn't hold a candle to Danny.

No one could.

CHAPTER 3

*M*ax Wallace slammed his door with a resounding *thud* that echoed around the inn and then immediately regretted it. Once again, he was allowing his temper to get the better of him—a temper he never used to have. He supposed failure did that to a person—turned them bitter, angry, an empty shell that spewed ugly words at everyone they came across in an attempt to hide that deep down, they were hurting. Badly.

Pull yourself together. Do you want everyone to know the truth?

He could hear Vanessa's voice as clearly as if she were standing beside him, whisper-snarling in his ear at yet another one of those awful society events she used to drag him to on an almost nightly basis.

His wife was all about keeping up appearances, something that grew harder with each passing day. Even though she dressed to the nines, dripping with designer clothes and diamonds, the truth was… they were drowning. Financially, emotionally, romantically.

She wouldn't even admit to her so-called friends that she and Max had separated some time ago, taking a break on a marriage that clearly wasn't working for either of them. Failure wasn't in her vocabulary—but to her, Max was just that, in every sense of the word. She'd told him enough times that he was starting to believe it. Not just believe it, but *live* it.

With a long, low sigh, Max returned to the writing desk he'd requested for the room and sank heavily into the chair behind it. He surveyed his work so far, which consisted of two lonely words on an otherwise blank page.

CHAPTER 4

*P*athetic, really, if he thought too much about it, which was something he tried to avoid at all costs. He used to sit down at the keyboard and the words would pour out of him as if by magic; these days, a chimpanzee would have an easier time stringing a sentence together. Maybe he really was a one-hit wonder. That's what the literary world was saying about him. That's what his agent was implying, whenever another year passed without a new manuscript.

His first book—his *only* book—had been successful beyond his wildest dreams, rocketing him into the stratosphere. A full-page writeup in *The New York Times*, several million copies sold, an option for a film that starred two of Hollywood's biggest names and earned a pair of Oscars to boot.

Then... nothing. When it came time to plan his second book, writer's block had hit him hard. But the panic hadn't set in until a year later, when the blank pages were still staring back at him, when his agent was beginning to ask pointed questions, when his wife was making increasingly frantic and accusatory comments about their dwindling bank account. Largely thanks to her out-of-control spending, he might add, but she never seemed to view it that way.

Things hadn't truly fallen apart, though, until the reality show cameras showed up.

He had begged her not to do it. Pleaded with her that his reputation as a serious author was on the line. That opening up their lives to the ridiculous antics of the women on that show would cause them far more problems than whatever paycheck it would provide. But Vanessa wanted her time to shine—in her words, she was tired of playing second fiddle to him, and she was going to sign that contract whether he liked it or not. He never actually expected her to go through with it, though, not when he was so adamantly opposed to it.

Apparently he didn't know her as well as he thought he did.

Vanessa quickly learned that the more dramatic, the more ridiculous, the more over-the-top her behavior, the more screentime she received—and therefore, the more money. She quickly became a fan favorite.

She quickly became someone he couldn't stand.

At least she had redeemed herself, somewhat, with the children's charity she had started. To date, she'd raised hundreds of thousands of dollars— possibly more—in search of a cure for childhood leukemia, even though Max could never be certain her actions were entirely altruistic. It had opened her up to a wider circle of socialite friends, many of them part of the ultra-elite, and Vanessa reveled in the attention. But the cause was worthy, and he wholeheartedly supported the endeavor. It was one of the few things in their dysfunctional marriage they were in agreement about.

In fact, the charity's most recent fundraising event was the last time Max saw his estranged wife before he packed his bags and left Manhattan for an extended vacation in Crystal Bay, where he hoped the scenery and solitude would help him recapture the magic that had been missing from his writing for so long. They had been playing the happy couple, as usual, with Vanessa begging him to keep up appearances as a condition of their formal separation. In reality, they barely spoke a word all evening, and when Max told her he was leaving the city for two months, she didn't even bother saying goodbye.

Which was fine. She may as well have been a stranger these days anyway.

Pulling himself out of his thoughts, Max stared at his computer again, willing the words to come. In the background, he heard the low laughter of the couple in the room next to him, and once more, he could feel his hackles rising—though he couldn't pinpoint exactly why. Maybe it was because they were too loud, breaking into his concentration at the exact time he needed to focus the most.

Or maybe it was because they were too happy.

He sighed. At least misery loved company. As a writer, he'd learned to watch the world around him, making observations in a way others didn't, filing them away for future perusal. So it hadn't taken him long to notice that the woman at the front desk— Audrey? Amelia? Avery? It didn't much matter—was just as unhappy as he was.

And for whatever reason, that brought him some

measure of comfort, as if she were a kindred spirit in this dark, lonely world.

Too bad he couldn't bring himself to at least be civil to her. He had a feeling hers was a story he very much wanted to hear.

"A DIVORCE LAWYER? So soon? Leah, I think you're making a big mistake."

Cynthia Hart set down her fork and shook her head in disbelief while Leah inwardly fumed, her eyes trailing to her sister, seeking backup.

"Mom, how can you say that?" Avery asked, her own fork clattering against her plate as she tossed it down in frustration. "After everything Phil did, I would think you'd be on Leah's side." The three women were eating dinner in the inn's kitchen at Avery's invitation, something Leah further regretted agreeing to with each passing moment.

"Of *course* I'm on Leah's side. What kind of mother would I be if I wasn't?" Cynthia's voice was dripping with faux patience, as if her daughters were the unreasonable ones. "I just don't want her to make a hasty decision that will have permanent consequences."

"I'm pretty sure Phil made the decision that had permanent consequences when he slept with Leah's best friend," Avery shot back, eyes dancing with anger. "Tell me, Mom, how many bonus children should he father before you deem it appropriate for Leah to leave him? Two? Five? A baker's dozen?"

"There's no need for sarcasm," Cynthia said coolly, cocking one eyebrow in her younger daughter's direction. "I'm merely worried that she's going to regret walking away from a twenty-five-year marriage in a matter of weeks. I think she should take some time to cool off, clear her head, and make a rational, well-informed decision about what she wants to do next."

"Yeah, well, I think she should dump him and take him to the cleaners." Avery attempted to spear a piece of broccoli on her fork with enough force to send it skidding across the plate. "I think she should make him pay for what he's done."

"Does anyone care what *I* think?" Up until now, Leah had been largely quiet, watching the back-and-forth between her mother and sister as if it were a tennis match she was only mildly interested in. Self-preservation, she supposed. Or exhaustion—anytime Phil's name came up, she wanted nothing more than to curl up under the covers and sleep away the pain of the past few weeks.

"Of course we do." Cynthia patted Leah's hand, which was about as much motherly affection as either of her daughters could expect from her. They secretly called her the ice queen, and speculated on how she could survive in sunny Florida without melting into a puddle in the sand, but in truth, she hadn't always been that way. Before Leah's father died, Cynthia had been a loving, attentive, playful mother who was always quick with a smile, a hug, or a kiss on a skinned knee. Her husband's death had changed her irrevocably, causing her to turn inward, shaving away her soft exterior to reveal a hardened, battle-weary woman underneath.

"We're just *concerned* about you, that's all," Cynthia continued, taking a dainty bite of meatloaf and chewing it much longer than was necessary. "I've barely slept a wink since you told me what happened. A mother worries, you know."

Leah studied her mother's face—her perfectly refreshed, well-rested face that was free of the dark circles that had plagued Leah since the day Phil had confessed to having a one-night stand with her best friend. "If you were worried about me, you'd stop questioning my decisions. It's the last thing I need right now—especially coming from you. I never even saw you and Daddy have an argument. You had the perfect marriage."

"No one has the perfect marriage." Cynthia's stylish gray bob swung back and forth as she shook her head adamantly. "Look no further than your own sister—we all thought she and Danny were the ideal match, and then he went off and found himself another woman."

"That is *not* what happened." Avery's cheeks reddened, and her hands balled into fists. "He didn't cheat on me. Why would you even imply such a thing?" Her voice cracked, and Leah rested a comforting hand on her arm, trying to convey silent support in the wake of their mother's casual cruelty.

"I'm not saying he *cheated*, per se. I'm just saying that he found that Molly woman awfully fast, don't you think?" Cynthia took a small sip of white wine, studying her younger daughter over the rim of her glass. "Suspiciously fast."

The look of raw devastation on Avery's face was too much for Leah to bear; instead, she brought the conversation back to herself. "There's no point in me dragging this out any longer. There's no point in giving Phil false hope. The marriage is done with, and was since the moment I discovered the truth.

There are some things you just can't come back from."

"And there are some decisions that can't be undone." Cynthia took a small sip from the glass of white wine she'd been nursing. "You can't expect Phil to stick around waiting for you to change your mind."

Leah gaped at her mother, her mouth opening and closing wordlessly. Then she pushed her plate aside and stood from the table. "I think I need to excuse myself from this conversation. Thanks for dinner, Avery. Let's not do it again."

Then, leaving her mother and sister staring daggers at each other, she strode out of the kitchen, making a beeline for the front door—and blessed freedom.

The sky was rapidly darkening, the air saturated with the scent of sea and sand. The first stars were twinkling in the dusky purple sky, and the last of the beachgoers were traipsing across the sand, umbrellas and chairs in tow, towels fluttering behind them in the wind kicking up off the water.

Leah drew her arms around herself as she made her way to the shoreline, kicking off her sandals and allowing the water to lap against her toes. A cluster of sand crabs scuttled past her, their iridescent bodies gleaming in the last rays of sunlight. In the distance, she could smell the first sparks of a beach bonfire, the hint of roasting marshmallows spiraling into the air. Closing her eyes, she could easily imagine that she was a teenager again, that she and Ben were sneaking out of their respective houses to meet up at the beach at midnight, to spend the darkest hours of the night talking and planning and dreaming. She'd lived for those moments, those magical nights when her future was stretched out before her, infinite in its possibilities. When she was young, the thought of what lay ahead being anything other than happy was... well, unthinkable.

Now, she had the benefit of time, and wisdom, and the knowledge that things didn't always work out the way you planned. When she and Phil exchanged vows on the day she considered one of the happiest of her life, she meant those words. She meant them to be forever.

Once upon a time, in the not-so-distant past, she would have believed that Phil had felt the same.

Did he still? Was she being too hasty?

Maybe her mother was right. Maybe they could overcome this. Maybe they could look back on this, years from now, as a terrible point in their marriage, but love and commitment and, most importantly, forgiveness had eventually dulled the pain. Made them stronger. More committed.

There was only one problem with that. Right now, the thought of looking him in the eye, knowing what he had done and how he had deceived her… it made her feel physically ill.

But could she overcome that too?

"Fancy seeing you here."

Leah's reverie was broken by a familiar voice, one that automatically soothed her, deep within her soul, and she turned to find Ben traipsing across the sand toward her. And he wasn't alone.

"Hey, Remi!" Leah was genuinely delighted to see Ben's younger sister. They had grown up as neighbors, and while Leah and Ben had become fast friends, the same could be said for Remi and Avery, who were born mere months apart. Their friendship had continued into adulthood, with Remi serving as the co-maid of honor alongside Leah at Avery and Danny's wedding.

"Leah." Remi gave her a curt nod that had Leah taken aback; there was no warmth in her expression, no welcome in her eyes. "I heard you were back in town for a while."

Leah faltered for a moment, glancing uncertainly at a pained-looking Ben, before saying, "Yes, for now, at least. I'm sure you know that Phil and I are separated."

Another curt nod, another blank look. Leah shifted uncomfortably in the sand, which was growing cooler as the sun slipped past the horizon. "I'm staying with Avery at the inn for a while, helping out," she continued. "Not that she needs me underfoot." She attempted a grin that fell flat as Remi turned from her to gaze out over the water, not bothering to respond.

By now, Ben's discomfort had morphed to annoyance, and he gave his sister's back a hard look before turning to Leah with a soft smile. "I'm glad we ran into you. I know you were having a hard time today... are you feeling any better?"

"I am. And thank you again for listening." Leah moved automatically toward Ben, and they both sank toward the sand in unison, their shoulders brushing. Remi turned her gaze from the cobalt sea just long enough to narrow her eyes at Leah, the expression there and gone so quickly she couldn't be positive she hadn't imagined it.

She glanced at Ben, whose expression was stone as he scooped up a handful of sand and let it trickle through his fingers. "Is everything okay?" she murmured, tucking up her knees and wrapping her arms around them. Overhead, a lone seagull soared over the shimmering water, dipping in and out of the waves as it searched for its dinner. In the distance, a single boat glided across the horizon, its occupants soaking up the last moments of twilight before slipping into the harbor.

"Everything's fine." Ben didn't meet her gaze; instead, he scooped up another handful of sand, allowing it to waterfall through his fingers once more. "Just tired, I guess. I've had a few long nights at the bar, and we haven't even hit summertime yet." He gave her a wry smile. "I think I need a vacation."

Leah laughed. "I never thought I'd hear those words coming out of your mouth. I thought Benjamin Grant didn't do vacations." Then, tipping her head up to the sky, her breath catching at the sight of the coral-streaked clouds, she murmured, "But now that you mention it, I could use a vacation myself." She nudged him playfully in the shoulder. "Where should we go? Tahiti? Bora Bora?"

"Anywhere." He met her eyes fully, and once again, her breath caught... but this time, it had nothing to do with the scenery. "I'll go anywhere with you."

She allowed herself just a moment to study his face, so beloved to her, and then she looked away, heart in her throat. After a beat, she attempted a playful response. "You say that now, but what if I decided I wanted to go backpacking through Antarctica? I'm not so sure a surfer boy like you could handle that."

He shrugged, a smile tugging at his mouth, his lips full and appealing. "Then I'll buy a coat."

Leah didn't know whether Remi had overheard their conversation, but the look of deep disgust she gave them once again took her by surprise. "I'm going to say hi to Avery," she said tersely. Then, ignoring Leah, she said to Ben, "Find me when you're finished with... whatever it is you're doing here."

Turning, she headed for the inn, kicking up clouds of sand as she walked, never once looking back, or saying goodbye to Leah, or even acknowledging her existence. After waiting until she'd wrenched open the inn's front door and disappeared inside, Leah gave Ben a bewildered look.

"Was it something I said? I haven't seen Remi in years... I can't imagine why she's acting so cold toward me."

"She's just..."

Ben trailed off, allowing the words to slip away into the darkness. Then he shrugged, but made no move to finish the sentence. Leah studied his profile —the square jaw, the spray of dark stubble across his cheekbones, the first lines of age creasing the corners of his mouth—then spontaneously took his hand in hers, feeling the warmth of his skin, the tingle that ran through her the moment they touched.

"Talk to me," she murmured. "Tell me what you're thinking. We're friends—you know you can tell me anything."

Something flickered across his face then—hurt? Disappointment? Leah couldn't be sure, but in the next moment, his expression had shuttered and he turned from her once more.

And though he remained by her side as the sky lapsed into darkness and the low roll of thunder rumbled in the distance, the air between them had shifted, growing thick with unease and an ocean's worth of words left unspoken.

CHAPTER 5

"*A*very, do you have a second to chat?"

Avery glanced up from the pillow she was wrestling into its case to find Molly hovering in the doorway to the guest room she was currently tidying up. Danny was feeling under the weather today, meaning Avery was solely in charge of preparing four of the inn's rooms for their next round of check-ins, which would be happening in less than two hours. The last thing she had time for was a chat... especially with Molly, who was currently clutching her wedding-planning binder and looking luminous.

"Of course." Avery set down the pillow with a smile. "What can I do for you?"

She gestured for Molly to enter the room, and

both women took seats on the end of the bed. Molly set the binder between them, then flipped it open and thumbed through the pages until she reached one marked "Ceremony."

"First of all, I just want to thank you for how wonderful you've been throughout this whole process," Molly gushed, tucking a strand of her red hair behind her ear and beaming at Avery. "From the moment Danny and I started dating, he's been singing your praises. And while I have to admit that I was hesitant to meet you—and intimidated, too, based on everything Danny had ever said about you —I've been blown away by your warmth and acceptance of our relationship. You've really been a true friend to Danny, and now to me, and that's something I'll always be grateful for."

As Molly was speaking, Avery felt herself go numb. Even though she knew it was inevitable—and natural—that she would come up in conversation between the couple, it felt like a betrayal on Danny's part all the same. As if her name on his lips in the presence of another woman was another nail in the coffin of their relationship, another swipe of the knife against the last threads of hope she held onto that he would come home.

But Molly was giving her an expectant look

now, clearly waiting for her to respond, and so it was with a strangled voice that Avery managed to choke out, "That's... nice. And you're welcome. Danny and I have worked hard to keep up a good relationship."

Well, she had, at least. Danny hadn't seemed like he needed to put the work in at all. For him, flipping the switch on their marriage—and sending her back to the friend zone, despite the years of intimacy they'd shared—had seemed as natural to him as breathing.

For Avery, it took work. The hardest type of work she'd ever experienced, day in and day out. Being civil to him after everything he had done was a choice.

Unfortunately, loving him was not. That was as natural to *her* as breathing.

"And it shows." Molly took Avery's hand and gave it a gentle squeeze. "I'm happy the two of you have such an incredible bond, and I can't wait for you and me to grow closer as well. I feel like we have a lot in common, and I'm eager to get to know you better. To become friends. True friends."

The numbness was spreading like wildfire, seeping into Avery's bones, twisting and writhing its way toward her heart. "That sounds lovely," she heard herself say, as if from a distance. "I'm sure we'll all get along great."

"I think so too." Molly bobbed her head eagerly, then withdrew her hand from Avery's and rested it on the binder. "Which is why I wanted to talk to you. Danny and I were thinking, since the three of us are going to be business partners, and more importantly, friends... we would love it if you would participate in our wedding ceremony. Nothing crazy," she said with a laugh. "We've already found a minister, but I thought maybe you could read a poem before we recite our vows? About love?" She flicked through the binder again, stopping on a single typed page that she passed to Avery. "It's by Walt Whitman, our favorite poet."

No, Avery wanted to scream. *No no no*. Walt Whitman wasn't *their* favorite poet. He was Avery's. An English major in college, she'd studied his works extensively, and introduced his words to Danny, poems of love and romance of such beauty that she used to whisper them into his ear when they were alone, entwined together in the darkness, their hearts beating as one. Their favorite line had even been inscribed on the inside of their wedding bands, a surprise from Avery to Danny that had his eyes welling up with tears when he first saw it.

And now Avery's eyes were welling up—with embarrassment, with grief, with a deep, bone-crushing loneliness over everything she had lost.

Seeing this, Molly gently removed the poem from Avery's hands and draped a comforting arm over her shoulders, then leaned forward to snag a tissue from the box on the nightstand. She offered it to Avery, who saw that her eyes, too, were glistening with unshed tears.

"I'm touched that this is making you so emotional," Molly said, procuring a tissue for herself and dabbing at her cheeks while Avery looked on, horrified that anyone could be so self-centered. And naïve. And completely, totally heartless. "I just know that this is going to be a beautiful part of the ceremony, and I speak for both Danny and myself when I say that we're honored to have you play such a special role in it."

Then, pulling Avery into a tight embrace, she whispered, "Thank you." Releasing Avery, she glanced around the room. "I won't keep you, I can see that you're busy... Do you need a hand?"

"No." The response was immediate; Avery glanced down to see that she had been quietly shredding the tissue in her hand. Shoving the pieces into her pocket, she stood, eyes lingering on the poem for a moment before she turned away, knot of sadness clogging the base of her throat. "No, that won't be necessary, but thanks for the offer. I'll see you around, okay?"

"Sooner than you think," Molly responded cheerfully, gathering her binder into her arms once more. "Now that we're holding the wedding here, I'll be dropping by with the caterer, the florist, the rental company…" She was ticking items off on her fingers as she spoke, then finished with a grin. "By the time I walk down the aisle, you'll be so sick of me you'll never want to see my face again."

Then she was gone with a wave and a wink, leaving Avery to stare at the empty doorway, mind blank with disbelief. Had the past five minutes happened? Had they actually *happened*? She would have thought she was dreaming—or having the world's worst nightmare—if not for the fact that the Walt Whitman poem was still lying on the bed, innocent on the surface but far more sinister upon closer inspection.

She picked it up, eyes scanning the page, the words she knew by heart.

She shouldn't have been surprised that they were the same ones engraved on their wedding bands. She shouldn't have been surprised by anything anymore.

Ten minutes later, she was still clutching the poem in her trembling hands when she heard footsteps bounding up the staircase. "Yoo-hoo, anyone here?" a voice called out, and a moment later, Avery's best friend Remi was poking her head around the doorframe, eyes lighting up at the sight of her.

"Hey there! I stopped by last night but heard you having an epic argument with your mother in the kitchen and thought I'd swing by today..." Then, catching sight of the expression on Avery's face, she faltered. "Is everything okay?" Her eyes trailed down to the poem, then back up to Avery. "What's that?"

Avery passed it to her wordlessly, watching through dull eyes as Remi scanned the words, her lips moving silently. Then, looking puzzled, she handed it back to Avery. "I don't get it. But something's obviously wrong, because you look like you've been dragged through the mud." Perching on the edge of the bed, she studied Avery with concern. "What's going on? Although I can probably take a pretty good guess." She sighed. "Danny?"

Avery nodded, still not trusting herself to speak. Then she rose abruptly from the bed, holding up a silent finger, signaling for Remi to wait. Exiting the guest room and descending the stairs, she pushed open the door to her and Danny's bedroom—*her* bedroom, she corrected herself, still not used to his absence despite the years that had passed—and opened the top drawer of her nightstand. There, tucked carefully in one corner of the drawer, nestled in a black velvet box, was her wedding ring, the white gold freshly polished and gleaming in the sunlight streaming through the window.

Gazing down at it for a moment, Avery tried to remember what the smooth band felt like on her finger, a constant reminder that she was loved, then lifted it from the box almost reverently. Cupping it in one hand, she climbed the stairs and found a bewildered-looking Remi sitting on the bed right where she had left her.

"What do you have there?" Remi asked, her voice edged with suspicion.

Avery opened her palm and let the ring fall to the bed. "Read the inscription," she said, then sat back and watched as Remi compared the words on paper to the ring's inscription. When she was finished, her brow furrowed into a frown again.

"I still don't get it. Why do you have this?" She waved the poem in Avery's face. "And why do you look like you want to slap someone?"

At this, Avery let out a genuine laugh, the first in what felt like years. "Not you, if that's what you're worried about." She swallowed hard, felt her voice beginning to crack. "Molly was just here. She and Danny have asked me to read this poem at their wedding ceremony. *This* poem."

Remi stared at her, comprehension dawning. Then, with a disgusted shake of her head, she said, "That's sick, Avery. That's actually sick. Tell me you're not going to go through with it." When Avery didn't respond, she leaned forward and grabbed her shoulders, forcing their eyes to meet. "Avery, seriously... tell me you're *not* going to go through with it."

"I... I don't know." Avery's voice was shaking as the full weight of the request hit her. "I didn't give her an answer, even though she seems to think I did." She gave Remi a desperate look. "How can I say no? How can I say *yes*?"

After falling silent for several moments, she whispered, "How can he be doing this to me? I don't understand, Remi, I honestly don't. Did he forget what this meant to us? Or does he just not care?" She shook her head, her dark hair flicking back and forth. "You know Danny—he doesn't have a cruel bone in his body. It's not like he's trying to hurt me."

"No, he would *never* do a thing like that." Remi's voice was heavy with sarcasm, and Avery flinched.

Admittedly, Remi wasn't the president of the Danny fan club, but what else could Avery expect from her best friend? She'd sobbed on Remi's shoulders countless times since she and Danny had split; if the situation were reversed, she would be equally furious on her friend's behalf. "My vote is for cruel," Remi continued, arms crossed tightly over her body. Then, relenting, she added, "Or stupid. Frankly, I think either description fits."

"Or maybe he's neither of those things." Avery's heartrate picked up as another thought, a *better* thought, occurred to her. She looked over at Remi, eyes shining with newfound hope. "What if he's confused? What if he's still in love with me, and just doesn't realize it? Or hasn't admitted it to himself yet?"

Remi looked stricken, eyes wide as she took Avery's hand in her own. "Oh, Avery. Oh, honey, I don't think—"

"It makes perfect sense!" Avery was on her feet now and pacing the room, her blood thrumming in her veins. "Think about it, Rem… Why would he choose *that* poem? Why would he want *me* in his wedding?" When Remi merely shook her head, eyes still wide, she said, "Because he hasn't let go of us. He hasn't let go of our marriage. He hasn't let go of *me*.

He still loves me, Rem—just like I always believed, in here."

She pressed a hand over her heart, stopping to gaze out the window at the shimmering sea. The beauty of the scenery before her took on a whole new meaning as the *rightness* of her realization took hold, burrowing into her soul, reigniting the flame of hope that had been nearly dead for so long. Danny still loved her. He still loved her... and he needed to know she felt the same. He needed a nudge in the right direction before he was married, and all was lost.

When she turned to Remi once more, she barely noticed her best friend's dismayed expression. Instead, she could feel her cheeks blossoming with color, her heart blooming with happiness, as she said, "I'm going to get him back. Are you with me?"

Remi was silent for several long moments, the air in the room thick with tension. Then, with a slow shake of her head, she said, "No, Avery... I'm not. I think... I think you're not seeing things clearly. I think you're letting what you want get in the way of reality. Danny has Molly now. They seem really happy together, and I know that's killing you. You have every right to be upset, but this... this isn't a good plan. It's only going to end in heartache."

"It won't," Avery said, eyes on the sea once more. In the distance, she could see a trio of dolphins diving in and out of the waves, the saltwater glistening off their backs. Suddenly she felt as carefree as them, and had a sudden urge to shed her skin and join them in their dance of joy. "It won't," she repeated, this time in a whisper that only she could hear. "You'll see."

"SORRY I'M LATE," Leah called to Ben as she kicked off her shoes and padded across the beach toward him, hastening her steps as the sand scorched the bottom of her feet.

The day was unseasonably warm, even for the Florida Panhandle, and Leah had donned shorts and a tank top, slathered her exposed shoulders in sunscreen, and pulled her blonde hair into a loose ponytail before meeting Ben for lunch. She had also chosen to go makeup-free, which would have been unthinkable when she was out running errands or meeting friends for a bite to eat in the city. Returning to Crystal Bay had allowed Leah to reacquaint herself with her roots, the simplicity and minimalism and connection to nature she hadn't realized she'd missed so desperately.

"I was just getting ready to start without you." Ben gestured to the bag of takeout food from Tom's Diner that he'd offered to pick up on his way to meet her, and as Leah caught the scent of perfectly greasy hamburgers and fries wafting out from the containers, she could practically hear her stomach growling in anticipation of a good meal.

"If you keep stuffing me with burgers and fries, I'm not going to fit into my pants," she teased, settling onto the blanket he'd spread over the blistering sand.

"Nah," he said, taking an enormous bite of his burger while she dug into her fries. He gestured toward the ocean, today a deep cerulean that reflected the cloudless sky. "The sea air keeps the weight off."

"Is that so?" A smile tugged at her lips as she tucked her legs beneath her and squirted a healthy dose of ketchup onto her burger. "Then I guess it's my luck to be living here again." She dipped a fry into the ketchup and popped it into her mouth, only noticing after swallowing that Ben was staring at her intently. "What?" she asked, suddenly self-conscious, her fingers trailing to her face to see if it was smeared with food but coming away clean.

"Are you?" he asked, the question in his eyes belying his nonchalant tone. He lowered his burger and studied her face, his eyes sweeping over hers, intense and probing.

She frowned at him, shifting uncomfortably under the weight of his scrutiny. "Am I what?"

"Living here again." By now, his food was lying forgotten in its container, a move so unlike Ben that Leah was taken aback. Normally he would have finished his burger in four bites and begun eyeing hers like a dog begging for scraps under the table. "Is that your plan?"

"For now."

"For now?" His disappointment was palpable, his eyes shadowed with uncertainty. "What does that mean?"

"It means... I don't know what it means." Leah shifted on the blanket so she could face him fully. "Everything that happened, it's still so new, so difficult to process. I can't predict what tomorrow will bring, let alone a month from now, a year... You get the picture." The sadness that flickered across his expression then was unmistakable, and Leah drew in a deep breath, knowing where the conversation had to go but dreading it all the same.

"I thought you said you would wait." Her voice was small, uncertain. "You know I'm not ready to jump into anything."

"I know that. And I will wait." Ben wasn't looking at her now; he had picked up a piece of seaweed that had washed to shore and was toying with it. "I have no problem waiting until you're ready. I just want to know that you'll *be* ready. Someday. I don't want to lose you again, Leah. I can't bear it."

She set her hand gently on his arm, forcing him to look at her. When he did, the expression in his eyes was raw and broken. "I can't bear it," he said again, reaching forward to brush his fingers along her cheek. Her eyes drifted closed at his touch, and those old feelings, the ones she had buried deep beneath the surface for so long, rose within her like tendrils of smoke. What would life have been like for her if she and Phil had never met? What would it have been like if she had stayed?

"Why didn't you ever tell me?" Her eyes were open again and focused on Ben. "You never said anything, you never gave me any indication that you had feelings for me."

If he had, would it have made any difference?

The answer was a resounding yes, even if Leah wasn't ready to admit that out loud. She had loved Ben for so long that she couldn't remember a time when she hadn't. But he'd never shown any interest in her, and when Phil came along, offering her the moon, she'd decided to take it. And why not? Without Ben, there was nothing for her in Crystal Bay, a town so small it was barely a dot on the map. She wanted to see the world. She wanted to experience *life*. She wanted to be loved, desperately.

"What can I say? I was young and stupid and thought I had all the time in the world." Ben let out a rough laugh, then flung the seaweed back into the water, where it quickly washed to shore once more. "I didn't anticipate Phil coming along. And I definitely didn't anticipate you up and leaving." The words were said simply, without accusation or bitterness. "I was completely blindsided. I guess I should have told you then, begged you to stay, but I didn't want to get in the way. I figured if you felt the same, you wouldn't have gone with him. Then, when you did... I knew I had my answer."

He glanced at her then, his face hesitant. After a long pause, during which the only sounds around them were the ocean crashing against the shore and the distant cry of a seagull, he said, "If I'd told you the truth, would anything have changed?"

The question launched Leah back to the past, back to the first time she met Phil. He had taken a summer job as a roofer in Crystal Bay, working on a house just down the road from hers. She walked by him every day on her way to work at the local ice cream shop, often exchanging a quick hello, her eyes wandering to his bronze skin, his wavy blond hair, his killer smile. He was undoubtedly charming, and from their first date onward, he'd treated her like a queen, like something precious and fragile and perfect. She'd fallen for him hard.

But Ben... oh, Ben. He was her beautiful boy, the one who made her heart race and her palms clammy. The one whose name was scrawled in every notebook and diary she had owned since the time she had learned to write. The one who held her heart in his hand, even if he hadn't known it. Her love for him had been so pure, a river that ran deep, a song constantly playing in her head. He had been her everything, and if he had asked... if he had told her... she would have dropped everything and run into his arms.

But loyalty to Phil, even now, even after everything, caused her to keep all of this inside. Instead, with a soft smile, she murmured to Ben, "That was such a long time ago. Who can say what any of us would have done? We were kids, Ben."

The disappointment in his eyes cut her to the core, and only after a very long pause did he nod and say, "Yeah, right, we were kids." With a deep inhale, he looked at her and added, "But we're not kids anymore, Leah. And I have to know, I have to ask, for my own sanity... Is any part of you planning on going back to Phil?"

There are some decisions that can't be undone. I'm worried you're going to regret walking away from a twenty-five-year marriage in a matter of weeks.

Her mother's words returned to her then, along with the uncertainty she'd felt after hearing them. Erasing so many years together, erasing a lifetime of memories, so many of them happy... it was a daunting prospect. She knew without a doubt that Phil would welcome her back with open arms, and she believed him when he said he was fully committed to working things out. The ball was in her court... but the game was something she never fathomed having to play in the first place.

"I see." Ben's voice was low, barely audible over the sounds of the sea. A sad smile was playing across his lips, a look of deep regret in his honey-brown eyes. "You don't have to answer the question. I understand."

He gazed down at his forgotten burger, expression vacant, as though he wasn't really seeing it. Then, standing and brushing the sand from his fingers, he said, "I just want you to know that I've regretted not telling you how I felt when I had the chance. I've regretted it every day of my life. How this has all played out… it's not your fault, it's mine."

And then he was gone, traipsing across the sand, head bent, shoulders stooped. Leah called after him, but her voice must have been lost to the wind, because he never turned back.

CHAPTER 6

"*A*very, please, I'm begging you to reconsider. This isn't a good idea."

Remi was standing in the inn's kitchen, arms crossed tightly over her chest, making a last stand against Avery, who was adding the finishing touches to a pot of chicken soup bubbling away happily on the stovetop. She was whistling as she worked, her cheeks pink from the steam rising from the pot, her heart light with anticipation, though the nerves were beginning to kick in as well.

"What's not a good idea? It's chicken soup, Rem. I'm not going to throw myself at him."

"Don't you think *Molly* should be the one making him chicken soup? You know, his fiancée?"

Avery flinched, then quickly recovered with a shrug. "She's not going to mind. He's sick, he's always loved my chicken soup, I just so happened to have all the ingredients..."

"You just so happened to run out and *buy* all the ingredients," Remi muttered, looking mutinous. "Seriously, Avery, have you ever just showed up at their house before? Have you ever actually stepped *foot* in their house?"

Avery paused in her stirring to consider the question. "No, I guess not. I've driven by it a few times, but I haven't been inside. That would have been weird."

"It's still weird!" Remi actually stomped her foot in frustration, causing Avery to stare at her, eyebrows raised. "Avery, you are not going to win him back over chicken soup. You are not going to win him back over anything. You should not even be trying to win him back! Need I remind you that he broke your heart, completely out of the blue, and then abandoned you? Need I remind you that he's been parading his relationship with Molly in front of you for years, even knowing how heartbroken you were after the divorce? Why would you even *want* a man like that?"

"No one's perfect." If Avery felt a twist of uncertainty in the face of Remi's points—all valid—she would never let it show. "Look." She turned to her best friend with a soft sigh. "I get that this must look insane to you, but Rem... this is my last chance. Don't you understand that? Danny is going to remarry in a matter of months. And if he knew how I felt... what if that changed things?"

"But he knew how you felt the first time around," Remi protested, blowing out a frustrated breath. "It didn't matter to him then, so why should it matter to him now?"

"I have to try. I can't live the rest of my life knowing that I didn't." Avery shot her friend an imploring look. "I'm not asking you to understand. I'm just asking for your support."

Remi's shoulders slumped in defeat, and she leaned against the kitchen counter, gnawing worriedly on her bottom lip. "I am trying to support you, Avery. I'm trying to support you by not sitting back and watching you get crushed. Again. By the same man who ripped out your heart and stomped all over it."

"Relationships aren't perfect." Avery murmured the words without really believing them. Her relationship with Danny *had* been perfect. Up until that last day, she had been deliriously happy. It had been perfect... until it wasn't.

Remi sighed again. "There's nothing I can say to stop you, is there?" she asked, shaking her head. "There's nothing I can say to make you change your mind?"

"Nope." Avery was bent over now, rummaging through the cabinets for a container and a lid. She emerged with them a moment later, then began ladling piping hot soup into the container. "Now if you'll excuse me, I have some soup to deliver."

Securing the lid on the container, she brushed past Remi on her way out of the kitchen and then ran straight into Max Wallace, who was headed for the front door, laptop tucked under his arm. "Sorry about that," he said as he reached out to steady the container in her arms as it wobbled precariously. "Didn't mean to almost knock you over."

The smile on his face disarmed her—up until now, she hadn't seen him look anything but surly. He sniffed the air. "Chicken soup? Smells amazing."

"I made it for someone special who's sick," Avery said, joining him as they headed down the hall toward the inn's foyer. When they arrived at the door, he held it open for her, waiting as she slipped on her shoes and stepped out into the sunshine.

"Shame to be sick on such a nice day," he said, setting his laptop on a coral Adirondack chair—Avery's favorite—and gesturing out at the cloudless sky. "I thought I'd try and get some work done out here for a change. The scenery stirs the creativity."

"But won't the seagulls be cawing too loud?" Avery gave him an innocent look, her annoyance at him melting away in her excitement over seeing Danny. To her surprise, he laughed, a full-body laugh that warmed her from head to toe.

"Still not as loud as the couple next door," he said with a grin. Then, wincing, he added, "I suppose I owe you an apology for being such an annoyance since I arrived at the inn. The truth is... I'm going through a tough time, and I'm taking it out on everyone else around me. So... I'm sorry." He held out his hand, ocean-blue eyes twinkling playfully. "Friends?"

"I don't know about friends," Avery teased, shifting the soup container to give his hand a firm shake. "How about innkeeper and guest?"

He laughed again. "I guess I can live with that. And despite all of my complaints, I just want you to know that you have a beautiful place here. One of the nicest I've ever stayed in. A true hidden gem."

"Thank you," Avery said, warmed by the compliment. She'd poured so much of herself, so much of her heart and soul into the inn, that any compliments it received felt personal. "I don't believe I've ever had someone stay for two months before. I hope that you still feel the same way when you leave."

Then, with a gracious smile, she thanked him again, leaving him to settle himself in the Adirondack chair and flip open his laptop. On the way to her car, she glanced back once to find him gazing out at the cerulean sea, his face troubled, but when he saw her, he plastered on a smile and offered a cheerful wave.

She returned it, then slipped into her car and started the engine, taking a moment to inhale a deep, steadying breath before making the short drive to Danny and Molly's house. As she navigated the car through Crystal Bay's humble back roads, which were lined with modest bungalows that boasted lush green yards with lemon, lime, and orange trees alongside beautiful blooms bursting with every color of the rainbow, she could feel herself white-knuckling the steering wheel. She hadn't expected Remi's support, exactly, but she also didn't anticipate her best friend being so vehemently opposed to the idea of her and Danny, either. Remi had a good head on her shoulders, and her reaction was giving Avery pause... until she pulled up to the curb in front of a cozy yellow bungalow and saw Danny through the window. At the sight of him, her heart somersaulted, and the knot of anxiety in her stomach eased.

This was right. *They* were right. They had more than twenty years of history to prove it.

Steeling herself, she checked her reflection in the rearview mirror, smoothing her hair into place and examining her teeth for food—not that she'd had any appetite today—before grabbing the soup container and making a beeline for the front door, projecting a confidence she certainly didn't feel. After a tentative knock, she stood back, heart pounding in her ears, and waited for Danny to open the door.

Which he did, several moments later, his brow furrowing when he caught sight of her standing there. "Avery? This... is a surprise."

Not the reaction she was expecting, but she could live with that. They had to start somewhere, right?

"I made you chicken soup." She shook the

container, drawing Danny's eyes to its contents. "I know it's your favorite, and I figured it would help you feel better." She gave him a shy smile. "The inn hasn't been the same without you." She passed the container to him, and he took it, still looking slightly baffled.

Then, glancing behind him, he said, "Uh, thank you. That's very kind. Would you... like to come in?" Raking his fingers through his dark hair, which was already standing adorably on end, he added, "I have to warn you, the place is a mess, and Molly isn't here right now, so..." He trailed off uncertainly, shifting from one foot to the other.

"That's fine, I don't mind."

Avery's heart was in her throat as she stepped around him and entered the house. Despite sharing countless hours working side by side at the inn, she and Danny hadn't spent any personal time together since several weeks before they'd signed the divorce papers. The idea of seeing him but being unable to touch him, or kiss him, or tell him how much she loved him—all of it a natural part of their life together—was more than she could stand. And Danny had never offered, presumably to give her the space she'd asked for. He'd purchased this house shortly after the divorce was official, but Avery had no idea when Molly had moved in. She hadn't asked. She hadn't wanted to know.

Now, as she entered the house, Avery was keenly aware that she was entering another woman's territory. Ignoring the large engagement photo hanging on the wall, featuring a grinning Danny and Molly gazing lovingly into each other's eyes, Avery gently removed the soup from Danny's hands and headed straight for the kitchen, opening and closing unfamiliar cabinets until she located a bowl and spoon.

"It's still hot," she said, pouring a generous helping into the bowl and offering it to him with another smile. "I just finished making it."

"Thanks, Avery, really. You didn't have to go through all this trouble. It's just a mild cold, and Molly has been taking good care of me."

He carried the bowl into the small dining room, motioning for Avery to follow him, and they settled themselves in chairs facing each other across the table. She watched intently as he lifted the spoon to his mouth, blew away the steam, and tasted the soup she'd spent all morning preparing, satisfied when he moaned softly in satisfaction... as she knew he would.

"This is delicious. I've missed it."

Six simple words, and they were enough to bring

tears to Avery's eyes. "I've missed making it for you," she murmured, tracing the tablecloth's delicate floral pattern with her fingers. She felt Danny's eyes on her face, but she didn't meet his gaze. Instead, still studying the table, she laughed softly and said, "Do you remember the first time I brought you some? You had that terrible flu and missed a week of classes."

"And then you insisted on kissing me and missed the next week." His laugh matched hers. "Although the chicken soup I made you wasn't nearly as good."

"Water, ramen noodles, and canned chicken that I'm pretty sure had expired a few months before you opened it." Avery smiled at the memory. "I didn't mind, though. It was a sweet gesture. That's when I knew you were the one."

Danny, who had been midway through lifting the spoon to his mouth, halted for a moment, leaving the spoon dangling in the air. He studied her, his dark eyes roaming over her face, and then he glanced down at his bowl once more. "This is delicious. Thanks again."

"You're welcome." Avery's voice was soft, tender, as she watched him enjoy the meal she'd prepared for him, something she'd done more times than she could count. No matter how busy their schedules had been, they always used to sit down at the end of the day and share dinner. Those were some of Avery's most cherished memories, the two of them on the inn's back patio, enjoying a meal as the sun painted spectacular colors across the darkening sky. Learning to eat alone was one of the hardest things she'd endured in the aftermath of their split.

Taking a deep breath, heart jack-hammering against her ribcage, she said, "Danny, I've been—"

"Hell-*oooo*! Honey, I'm home! How's my darling boy feeling—"

Molly stopped short when she entered the dining room and saw the two of them sitting at the table. Avery sat frozen, smile fixed on her face, familiar numbness creeping over her once more.

"Avery! What a wonderful surprise. What are you doing here?" Molly's eyes scanned the table, zeroing in on the soup. "Oh, did you make that for Danny? Aren't you the sweetest thing."

"Yeah, well, the inn isn't the same without..." Avery trailed off as Molly settled herself in Danny's lap, arms wrapped around his neck. She gave him a soft kiss on the lips, then pressed her hand to his forehead.

"How are you feeling, baby? You seem a little warm."

"I'm fine. Probably just the soup." He smiled at her, but Avery could see that he looked distinctly uncomfortable. Extricating himself from Molly's arms, he said, "I am feeling a bit run-down, though. I think I'll take a quick nap."

"Of course. Avery and I will catch up for a bit, won't we? Have a little girl time?" Molly grinned at her, and Avery felt her heart plummeting to somewhere in the vicinity of her feet. This was *not* how today was supposed to go. Not even close.

Gently removing Molly from his lap, Danny stood and stretched, his T-shirt riding up over his flat, tan stomach. Avery caught herself admiring him… and then glanced over and saw Molly doing the same. "Thanks again, Avery, for the soup. You're awesome. And your little trick worked."

"Trick?" Avery felt her throat go dry, felt Molly's eyes on her face.

"Yeah, your trick to get me back to work as soon as possible." He gestured to the soup. "A few more bowls of that and I'll be back on my feet in no time."

"Oh." Avery let out a hollow laugh. "Good. Great. So I'll see you tomorrow, then?"

"You betcha." He offered her one last smile. "I'll see you later, okay?"

Avery raised her hand in a half-hearted wave as

he traipsed out of the dining room, leaving her and Molly alone at the table. The silence that fell over them was thick with awkwardness—for Avery, at least. Molly, for her part, gave her an easy smile and said, "You will stay for a cup of tea, won't you? It's the least I can offer after you were so sweet to Danny."

"Oh, I'd love to, but I really need to get back to the inn. We've got a full house right now." She slipped her cell phone out of her pocket and checked the display to see if any of the guests had tried to contact her—she provided them with her phone number during the rare times when the front desk was unmanned.

No missed calls or messages, although Molly didn't need to know that. With a loud sigh, she said, "Yep, just as I suspected... everyone seems to need me the second I step away." She rose from the table. "I'll just let myself out. Thanks for the hospitality."

"Thank *you*," Molly said cheerfully, not a hint of suspicion in her eyes. Not a hint of wondering why Danny's ex-wife had shown up at her house in the middle of the day. Not a hint of mistrust or apprehension. It was as if Avery were Danny's sister, or mother, or someone equally unthreatening, and not a woman who had years of shared history, years of shared intimacy, with him.

To Molly, Avery was a nobody.

But not for long.

"LEAH? Is it okay if you and I talk for a few minutes?"

Leah glanced up in surprise to find Remi standing outside her room at the inn, hands shoved awkwardly in her pockets, the gesture so reminiscent of Ben that she had to hide a smile.

"Of course," she said, pointing to the neatly folded pile of clothes beside the open suitcase propped on the bed. "I was just packing for my trip back home." The last word gave her pause, accompanied by a feeling of unease in her stomach—she was used to thinking of the city as her home, but right now, she was a woman in limbo.

If Remi noticed her hesitation, she made no mention of it. Instead, she said, "Oh, right, Ben mentioned you were leaving. Sorry, I'll just catch you when you come back, okay?" She began backing out of the doorway, but Leah stopped her with a shake of her head.

"I've got plenty of time. Come in, make yourself comfortable." She smiled at Ben's younger sister. "I'd normally offer you something to drink, but I'm afraid I'm a little short on refreshments at the moment. I won't rat you out to Avery if you decide to raid the inn's refrigerator, though. Not that she'd mind. You're pretty much her favorite person in the world."

Remi offered her a weak smile as she stepped into the room. "Not right now, I'm not. Which is what I wanted to talk to you about." She leaned against the windowsill, the sun's rays illuminating her dark hair, bringing out hidden highlights of red and gold. "I'm worried about her."

Leah frowned at Remi, sinking onto the bed opposite her and giving Ben's sister her full attention. "What do you mean?"

"I don't know if I should be telling you this, but…" Remi hesitated, her eyes on the ceiling as she debated what to say next. Then she sighed. "Avery has it in her head that Danny is still in love with her but just doesn't know it. Her plan is to win him back."

She glanced at her watch. "Right now, she's at his house, plying him with chicken soup and presumably stories about the good old days, all under the guise of helping him when he's sick."

She toyed with the ends of her long hair. "I'm really concerned about her, Leah. This whole thing with Danny has done a number on her... and I'm afraid with the wedding coming up, the stress is causing her to dive right off the deep end." She shook her head. "The whole thing is so sad."

"It is," Leah acknowledged in a soft voice. "It definitely is." She sighed, long and low, and turned her eyes to the horizon. "I can still remember the first time Avery introduced us to Danny. She was on cloud nine—she was positive he was the one. And we all loved him, of course... funny, handsome, friendly. Who wouldn't fall in love with him? During their marriage, every time I talked to her, she always seemed so happy. I was shocked when I found out that Danny had asked for a divorce, and even though Avery has put on a brave face in the years since, I know it's been killing her. The loss of him, the loss of the family she wanted so badly... I can't blame her for holding on to false hope."

"But it's not good for her," Remi said, her tone suddenly sharp. Then, with a deep breath of her own, she added, "It's preventing her from moving on." She looked away from Leah then, anger flitting across her pretty features.

Leah, noticing this, studied Remi's face for a long moment before saying, "You're not just here because of Avery, are you?"

Remi swung back to face her again. "What do you mean?" she asked, her voice almost confrontational. "Of course I'm here about Avery."

"You're also here about Ben." Leah settled her hands in her lap and stared at his younger sister intently. "You're worried he's going to get hurt… that I'm going to hurt him."

Remi opened her mouth and then closed it again, lost for words. She remained quiet for several long moments, the air thick with tension, until finally her shoulders slumped and she exhaled softly.

"I am worried about Ben. I don't think you'd hurt him intentionally, but it took him years to recover the last time, Leah. *Years.* I watched him wait for you, I watched him hope you'd return, I watched those hopes completely dashed when the wedding invitation showed up in the mailbox. I begged him not to go, but he wanted to support you. And when he came home the next day, after watching you and Phil together… he was a broken man. It took him a long time to come to terms with losing you, and now that you're back, I see that same hope in his eyes once more. And Leah, I can't bear to see him break again."

As Remi spoke, Leah's eyes filled with tears. Of sadness for her friend? Of regret for what could have been? Over fear for what might happen now? Maybe some combination of the three. All she knew was that hurting Ben, causing him pain, then or now, was the absolute last thing she ever wanted to do. And when she said that to Remi, Ben's sister nodded.

"I know. And I also know you're a good person, Leah, and probably don't deserve the cold shoulder I gave you the other night on the beach. But Ben is important to me, and I can't stand seeing him get hurt. Things between you and Phil are complicated, and rightfully so, but I think Ben has it in his mind that your separation is a done deal. That you and Phil are over for good, and that he might be able to make amends for not telling you how he felt all those years ago."

"I'm not sure he thinks that anymore," Leah said, mind wandering back to her and Ben's disastrous lunch on the beach. The hurt in his eyes, the defeat in his posture when he walked away... it wasn't something she would soon forget. "And as for me and Phil being done, that's the plan. I don't feel like our marriage can come back from what's happened, but..."

She ran her hands roughly through her blonde hair as she blew out a frustrated breath. "It's not so simple, I guess. The last time I saw him, I was positive things were over. But the doubts are beginning to creep in, brought on by fear, I guess, of the unknown. Of what's going to happen in the future. I'm in my late forties, and suddenly, I'm alone."

"You're not alone," Remi insisted. "You have your family, you have Ben, you have the Crystal Bay community...and you have me." She offered her a shy smile. "If you're not furious with me for the way I've treated you, that is."

Leah laughed. "I'm not. And I understand, believe me. Seeing what's happened with Avery has awoken a new kind of fury in me. We're protective of the ones we love, and there's no fault in that."

"No, I suppose not." Remi's gaze drifted out the window once more, to an older couple strolling along the sand, hand in hand, while a golden retriever puppy bounded ahead of them. The dog's coat was gleaming in the sunshine, tongue lolling happily, tail wagging in ecstasy as she bounded in and out of the waves. "Which brings me back to Avery. What should we do?"

Leah shook her head. "I'm not sure there's much we *can* do, but the next time I see her, I'll talk to her. I just hope she doesn't get her heart crushed in the meantime."

"I think her heart is already crushed." Remi swallowed hard, tears forming in her eyes on behalf of her friend. "Let's just hope that this time, she can come back from it."

AVERY STILL HADN'T RETURNED to the inn by the time Leah's suitcase was packed and sitting by the front door. She had taken her time getting ready so that she could speak to her sister before she left—at least that was what she kept telling herself.

In reality, she was stalling, big time. The family dinner was planned for the following evening, but Leah had decided to stay in the city for the weekend to grab some more of her belongings from the house and tie up a few loose ends. She also planned to have lunch with a couple of her friends, who had sent her more than a few texts asking if she was okay. She'd largely left them unanswered… because what was there to say? She was very much not okay, and probably wouldn't be for a long time.

But by now, the day was fading to twilight, and Leah knew that if she wanted to get to her hotel by midnight, she needed to leave now. So after scrawling a quick note to Avery telling her she'd see her in a few days, she stepped outside into the balmy evening air, which was tangy from salt and sand and a hint of fish that was not at all unpleasant.

As she was wrestling her suitcase out the front door—she'd packed way too many outfits, having no idea what one should wear when preparing to face their soon-to-be ex-husband for the first time in weeks—she heard her cell phone chime with an incoming text. Setting down her suitcase, she slid the phone out of her pocket and swiped her finger over the screen to read the message, heart leaping into her throat when she saw it was from Ben.

Sorry for the other day—I was being a jerk. Hope everything goes well with your family. If you need me, you know where to find me.

Just as Leah was preparing to type out a response, the phone chimed again with two more words.

Still friends?

Leah laughed, imagining him in that moment— the way his dark hair curled over his forehead when it got too long, the softness in his honey eyes whenever he looked her way, his strong, reassuring presence that always made her feel safe, no matter what problems she had in her life. He was her rock, her safe place, and in many ways, her home.

Still friends, she typed back, then slid her phone back into her pocket and grabbed her suitcase once more.

And this time, it was with a smile on her lips and a newfound lightness in her heart.

CHAPTER 7

"*I*s everything okay? I don't want to pry, but you've looked upset every time I've passed you this morning."

Avery glanced up from the desk with bleary eyes to find Max Wallace standing a few feet away, looking down at her with concern. His laptop was tucked under one arm, a beach towel under the other, and a smear of sunscreen was still visible on his nose. He gestured toward the window, where an impossibly blue sky awaited.

"I was just headed down to the beach for a little while, if you'd like to join me? Get your mind off your troubles?"

He gave her a kind smile, which was almost enough to cause Avery to break down completely.

She'd been a wreck since returning from Danny's house yesterday, the loneliness only compounded when she realized her sister had left for a few days. In all the commotion, she'd entirely forgotten she'd have the inn to herself this weekend.

Well, almost to herself. There was Danny, of course, who looked well-rested and chipper, thanking her repeatedly for the chicken soup. And Molly, who was clinging to his arm like an amorous parrot, following him everywhere he went, talking loudly to anyone and everyone in earshot about her plans for their wedding. Which would, apparently, include their very own fireworks show over the water, a gift from Danny's parents.

When Avery and Danny had wed, his mother had given her bathroom towels. Purple and orange, the ones stuffed in the bottom of the discount bin at the local home goods store.

"I'm fine, but thanks for asking. Just a rough night."

Indeed, Avery had tossed and turned for hours until finally sitting up in bed and flicking through the television channels. Then she'd spent the darkest hours of the night binge-watching *Society Wives*, the reality show that featured Max's wife, Vanessa. And boy, was that woman a piece of work—starting fights, overturning furniture, bragging about her designer clothes and vacation home in the Hamptons. She was as fake as they came, and it fascinated Avery to no end that a man seemingly as reserved as Max Wallace was married to someone so… hysterical.

"Well, if you're sure." Max smiled down at her again, and again, the gesture warmed her heart. Perhaps she had been wrong about this one.

"My sister tells me you're a world-famous author." Avery was suddenly feeling conversational, but she hadn't anticipated his face to freeze, or his eyes to harden. "I'm sorry," she said, taken aback. "Did I say something wrong?"

It took a moment for him to respond, and then, "No." He sighed. "No, you didn't say anything wrong. It just touches a sore spot, that's all." He gave her another smile, though this one didn't quite reach his eyes. "I *was* a world-famous author, I suppose you could say. Right now, I'm considered more of a one-hit wonder."

He held up his laptop. "That's why I'm here, in fact. I thought some beautiful weather and a little solitude would help me break through the writer's block I've been experiencing the past couple of years. According to my agent, if I don't produce a viable book in the next few months—and by viable, she means sellable—my contract with the publisher will fall through and my career will effectively be over."

"Oh, wow," Avery murmured. "I'm sorry to hear that." Then she brightened. "But if it makes you feel any better, *I* still think you're a world-famous author."

"You've read my book?" He looked deeply flattered, and Avery winced.

"Not quite. Not that I haven't wanted to, of course," she added hastily, even though she had no clue what the title was, or the foggiest idea what it was about. "Sadly, I don't have much time for reading these days. But you managed to write a successful book, and make a living off of it. That's pretty rare, I understand."

"Thank you for being so gracious." Max inclined his head. "We writers tend to have massive egos, and we bruise easily. Your words... they help, especially now."

He was leaning against the desk now, blue eyes studying her face in a way that made her feel distinctly uncomfortable... but in a not-altogether unpleasant way. A lock of his salt-and-pepper hair had fallen across his forehead, and Avery had a fleeting feeling that she'd like to reach over and brush it back.

Whoa. Where had *that* come from?

Married, she reminded herself. Married married married.

And besides, she was in love with Danny. So there was that.

He chose that moment to walk by, with Molly still clinging to him—why was she always *hanging* on him?—and Avery felt her own face freeze. Max, noticing this, glanced Danny's way and then back to her, his expression softening with understanding.

"Ah. You love him," he said when they were out of earshot.

Avery let out a hollow laugh. "It's more complicated than that. I used to be married to him."

Max was quiet for a moment, almost introspective, and then he said, "I see." Then, straightening, he added, "If you ever need someone to talk to, I've been told I'm a very good listener."

"There's that writer's ego again." Avery gave him a sly smile, warmed once more at the sound of his laughter, rich and deep. "But thank you. I appreciate that." She gestured to his arms, still weighed down by his laptop and beach towel. "Good luck with the writing. And enjoy this beautiful day."

"You too." There was that smile again, boyish and charming, though it flickered when Danny's laughter echoed down the hallway. "And good luck to you, too," he added, as suddenly Avery felt exhausted, down to her very bones. He strode toward the front door and was gone a moment later, though she watched through the window as he walked toward the sand, his T-shirt billowing in the warm breeze lifting up from the water.

"He's handsome, isn't he?"

Suddenly Molly was beside the desk, grinning down at her, eyes sparkling with amusement. She nodded toward the window, toward Max's retreating back. "Give him a couple of years, and he'll be a silver fox." Leaning across the desk, she whispered conspiratorially, "Want me to put out some feelers, see if he's single?"

"He's not." Avery's tone was curt. "And besides, I don't get involved with the inn's guests. It's bad form."

Molly shrugged; if she'd noticed the steel in Avery's voice, she gave no indication of it. "I don't see why not. Crystal Bay is such a small town, it's hard to find someone. It was just pure luck when I met Danny." She turned doe eyes on the man they both loved, who was visible through the kitchen doorway, whistling as he tinkered with the leak that had sprouted up beneath the sink. Then, rapping her knuckles once on the desk with finality, she said, "If you change your mind, let me know. I'm a *very* good matchmaker."

"I'll do that." Avery had to work hard to keep her breathing under control. Then she graced Molly with a practiced smile. "Thank you."

"You're welcome." Then, laughing as they both heard a *thunk*, followed by the sound of Danny swearing, she said, "I'd better go rescue him from himself. Honestly, the man has two left hands, doesn't he?"

"He does," Avery said softly, wistfully, though once again, Molly failed to notice. Or didn't care. Why should she? She had everything she wanted—which just so happened to be everything Avery wanted, too.

The phone rang then, just the distraction Avery needed, and Molly slipped away as she picked up the receiver, balancing it between shoulder and ear as she said, "The Inn at Crystal Bay. Good morning, this is Avery, how may I help you?"

"Good morning," a woman said in a businesslike tone. "My name is Samantha Goodall from Miami's

Channel 7 News. I was wondering if you had a guest named Max Wallace staying with you?"

"I'm sorry," Avery said, frowning into the phone, "but it's against our policy to give out the names of our guests. I'm afraid I can't help you." Then she set down the receiver with a soft *click* and stared at it for a moment, wondering why a news reporter would be trying to track down Max.

UNLIKE THE LAST time Leah returned to the house she and Phil had shared, he kept his word, and made himself scarce. She double-checked the driveway, and then every car up and down the street, before letting out a sigh of relief and parking at the curb in front of the beautiful gray stone house she'd called home for so long. It was with a sense of trepidation that she slotted the key in the front door and pushed it open, the familiar sights and scents of her home almost overwhelming her as she stepped inside. She took a moment to admire it—every loving detail she'd added, every knick-knack and decoration she'd chosen over the years. All the ways, big and small, that she had transformed it from a house into a home.

Then, so as not to let the memories overcome her, she walked purposefully up the stairs and to her room, taking care not to glance at the bed she and Phil had shared. Instead, she headed for the closet and en-suite bathroom to gather up a few of the belongings she hadn't yet brought with her to Crystal Bay, then marched out of the room, down the stairs, and out the door without looking back. She had no desire to stay in the house for more than a few minutes. Her children were gone, she and her husband were estranged; there was nothing for her there any longer.

Fortunately, lunch with her friends—sans Kate, of course—was just what the doctor ordered, and ten minutes later, she was pulling open the restaurant's front door and waving enthusiastically to them when she spotted them huddled at a nearby table. They immediately waved back, and though they looked happy to see her, something about their faces—guilt?—had her hesitating, had her positive that they had just been talking about her.

Not that she could blame them, really. These days, her life closely resembled a soap opera.

Swallowing back her unease, she approached the table and slid into the seat they had saved for her.

"Hi, ladies," she said, smiling at Carla, Opal, and Dana in turn. "How's it going?"

"Forget about how we're doing. How are *you*?" Carla's green eyes were shadowed with concern. "You left town so quickly, we had no idea what happened. Then we heard some things..." She trailed off, glancing at the other two for support.

Opal nodded. "We heard about Phil and Kate." Her blue eyes were owl-like, too large for her thin face. "Oh, honey, I couldn't believe my own ears. It's positively horrible."

"Disturbing," Dana agreed.

"Despicable," Carla chimed in.

"He's a cad. And she's even worse." Opal rested a delicate hand on Leah's wrist. "And Jace? I know you treated him like one of your own, Leah. You must be absolutely devastated."

Leah's heart sank at the mention of Jace. She loved Kate's boy fiercely, and had since the day he was born. She had been present for every milestone in his life, and he had bestowed her with the honorary title of "aunt." Her husband was always "Uncle Phil," too, though she distantly wondered if that had changed.

Did Jace know the truth? Was he as blindsided as

Leah? He was far too young, far too vulnerable and impressionable, to be caught up in this mess.

The others must have seen the sadness painted across Leah's face, because Opal quickly changed the subject. "So tell us about Crystal Bay—you're staying with your sister?"

"Yes, at her inn." Leah reached for the pitcher of water and poured herself a glass. "It's a beautiful place, an old Victorian house that she and her business partner fixed up. It's right on the water, the most beautiful crystal-clear water you've ever seen. And the beaches have white sand and stretch for miles in all directions…" Leah found herself smiling, a genuine smile, one that was already tinged with wistfulness. She had only left Crystal Bay last night, but her soul was already pining for it.

"That sounds amazing." Carla sighed. "We'd better visit you there while we can—right, ladies?"

The others all nodded their agreement, but Leah found herself frowning. "What do you mean, while you can?"

"Well, we expect you'll only be there another week or two at the most, right?" Dana glanced around at the other two for support. "I mean at some point, you'll come home. You and Phil will work this out, things will return to normal."

Leah let out a small, quiet laugh. "I don't think things will ever be 'normal' again. And as of right now... I have no plans on leaving Crystal Bay."

"No plans on leaving? Isn't that town, like, miniscule?" Carla was staring at Leah in disbelief. "Does it even have a *mall*?"

Leah gave her friend a bemused look. "No, it doesn't have a mall. But it has the beach."

"How long can you spend on the beach?" Carla wrinkled her nose delicately. "With all that sand everywhere..." She grinned. "Frankly, I'd much rather be shopping." Then, leaning across the table, she said, "But seriously, Leah, when are you coming home? You aren't cut out for small-town life. Phil can give you everything you need. Everything *any* woman needs. Money, security, a roof over your head, fancy vacations..."

She was ticking items off on her finger while she talked. "Sure, he cheated, and it was awful of him to do that with your best friend, of all people. But don't, like, twenty percent of men cheat? At least? It's almost like a natural thing for them. It's biological."

By now, Leah was staring at her friend, mouth agape. "It's bio*logical*? Whatever happened to loyalty? Whatever happened to commitment? That's what I signed up for. That's what I deserve. I don't care how many men cheat—my husband wasn't supposed to be one of them. He was supposed to love me unconditionally."

The three women exchanged dubious looks before Opal said quietly, "I mean, it would be great if it was actually like that, wouldn't it? But I don't know too many women who have a marriage like that. You all know that Don had a little... thing... with his secretary a few years back, right?" Leah and the others nodded solemnly. "I thought about leaving. Who wouldn't, right? But then I decided being alone—or worse, having to date again in my late forties—seemed way worse than reconciling. And we have... for the most part." She sighed. "I don't trust him completely, but at least I have someone to eat dinner with every night."

"After that whole nanny incident, Steven and I developed a little 'don't ask, don't tell' policy." Carla was studying her perfectly manicured nails. "He doesn't ask me questions, and I do the same for him." She shrugged. "It works for us."

"Well it doesn't work for me. I want someone who only wants me, and I don't think that's too much to ask."

Ben's face flashed through Leah's mind then, his expression of deep sadness when she couldn't give him the answer he wanted about her future with Phil. She knew, with profound certainty, that he would never stray. He would never make her question his feelings for her. He would never make her feel... less than.

"There's one other thing." Dana took a deep breath and glanced at the other two, who hesitated before nodding. The three of them turned to Leah, expressions identically grave.

"What?" she asked nervously.

"Well, take this with a grain of salt, of course, because none of us have seen it with our own eyes... but the rumor around the neighborhood is that Phil and Kate have been seeing quite a bit of each other these past few weeks." She winced. "We debated whether to tell you, because we don't want to meddle, but... we thought you had a right to know."

Leah's blood ran cold while her mind raced to find an explanation for what she had just heard. Because there *had* to be an explanation, right? She cast around for one, and then, with a sigh of relief, her thoughts settled on Jace. Of course. Kate and Phil had no choice but to see each other—they shared a child together, a child who probably knew the truth by now. As much as she despised both of them for what they did, Leah would never begrudge

Jace the chance to finally have an actual father in his life.

When she shared this theory with her friends, all of them exchanged one last look before Opal nodded vigorously. "That makes *perfect* sense, Leah," she said, her hand on Leah's wrist once more. "I'm sure that's exactly what's going on. Don't go listening to silly gossip—you're above that." Then, picking up the menu, she scanned her eyes down it and said, "Who's ready to eat?"

CHAPTER 8

$\mathscr{L}$eah was still trying to shake her unease over Phil's reported contact with Kate when she stepped into the restaurant that evening, nervously smoothing the nonexistent wrinkles on the simple navy dress she'd chosen for the occasion. When she glanced around the crowded waiting area, she immediately spotted her son Andrew, who was standing off to the side, scrolling through his cell phone.

Seeing her, he immediately slid the phone into his pocket and greeted her with his trademark bear hug that instantly melted her worries. "Hey, Mom." He pulled back and kissed her on the cheek, blue eyes scanning her face. "How are you doing?"

"I'm doing fine. Glad to see you, mostly." She

pressed her palm to his cheek, marveling, as she always did, that the boy she had raised had somehow become a man in the blink of an eye. He was looking more and more like Phil with each passing year, and she could see some of the other twenty-something women in the room watching him with an appreciative eye. "How have you been?"

"Okay, I guess." He shrugged, though his eyes looked troubled. "Upset with Dad, mostly. I'm having a hard time wrapping my brain around what happened." Lowering his voice, he added, "Callie doesn't know about Kate yet, right?"

"Right," Leah confirmed. "I know I have to tell her, but the timing hasn't been right yet. You know how much she adores and idolizes your father. It's... delicate."

"Frankly, I don't know how I'm going to look him in the eye tonight." Andrew's expression turned stormy. "He's tried calling me more than once in the past few weeks, but I haven't been able to bring myself to answer. I'm too angry. You're the last person who deserves this, Mom."

Leah shook her head, though she was touched that her son was so willing to defend her. "I'm fine, honey—really, I am. What I want most is for tonight to go smoothly. I know this is important to Callie, and no matter what happens between me and your father, we have to learn to get along. So please, for Callie—and for me—let's keep things as normal as possible, okay?"

Andrew studied her face for a long moment, then gave her a reluctant nod. "Okay. For you."

"Thank you." Leah turned toward the door just in time to see Callie arrive with Jeremy, her daughter looking radiant as the two of them walked arm in arm into the restaurant. Her smile slipped slightly as she saw Phil enter a few steps behind them, looking as handsome as ever in a blazer and dark blue button-down that perfectly comple-mented his eyes.

He glanced around the restaurant, and when his gaze met hers, the entire restaurant melted away—in that moment, there was only the two of them, familiar yet strangers in so many ways. Leah's heart was beating so rapidly with nerves that she felt dizzy, and the look of longing in Phil's eyes was unmistakable. He raised a hand in greeting, and Leah, swallowing hard, glanced away.

This was going to be much, much harder than she'd anticipated.

Andrew took a protective step toward his mother as Callie, noticing none of this, made a beeline for

Leah, her expression one of pure happiness as she gestured to Jeremy. "Mom, Andrew, this is Jeremy."

Leah greeted him warmly while Andrew offered him a handshake, and as Phil wove his way through the crowd, she said to Callie in as casual a voice as she could muster, "Here comes your father. I'm sure he's dying to meet Jeremy."

Was it her imagination, or did Callie suddenly look shifty? Her suspicions were confirmed a few moments later when, with a glance at Jeremy, Callie said, "Actually, the three of us have already been out to lunch a couple of times. You know, with Dad being alone here and all, I thought he could use the company…"

She trailed off with a nervous look at Leah, who quickly arranged her expression into one of nonchalance, though the news brought with it an arrow of pain aimed directly at Leah's heart. She wasn't expecting her daughter to choose her side; in fact, she adamantly didn't want her to. But to think that her sweet girl was automatically sympathizing with her father, while simultaneously drawing Leah as the villain, brought about a feeling of betrayal that rivaled how she felt about Phil.

Choosing not to respond—and fearing she might break down if she did—Leah merely stepped aside as

Phil joined the group, greeting Jeremy with an enthusiastic handshake, as if the two of them were bosom buddies. "Jeremy, my boy! Good to see you." He wrapped Callie in a hug, then clapped a frosty-looking Andrew on the back before turning to Leah, eyes softening.

"Hi there." He bent down to kiss her on the cheek. "You look great."

"Thanks." Leah forced herself to meet his gaze, her smile tight, and clenched her hands into fists to prevent herself from wiping away the imprint of his lips on her skin. "You look well too, Phil."

His smile flickered at the coolness in her tone, but he quickly recovered and took charge, striding up to the hostess to let her know that their entire party had arrived for their reservation. A few moments later they were being led to a table in the back corner of the restaurant, where an awkward shuffling of feet took place as everyone found their seat.

Despite her best attempts, Leah found herself sitting across from Phil, and she quickly picked up a menu and buried her nose in the wine list to avoid having to make small talk. Andrew, seeing this, engaged his father in a long-winded discussion about his job as a software engineer at a tech startup while Callie and Jeremy whispered together, heads bent toward each other, completely oblivious to the rest of the world around them.

Leah watched them with a sad smile playing around her lips, remembering a time when she and Phil had looked at each other like that—with complete devotion, tireless love. When had it all gone wrong? When she returned her attention to her menu, the conversation between Phil and Andrew had ended, and she could feel her husband's eyes on her face. Reminding herself that the goal for tonight was civility, she set the menu aside and met his gaze.

"How are you?" he asked softly. His hand twitched, as though he was longing to reach for her, and she curled her own hands in her lap. "I've missed you."

"I'm fine," she responded, ignoring his last words. "Keeping busy with Avery at the inn, catching up with my mother. It's been good being back in Crystal Bay. I hadn't realized how much I've missed it."

A shadow flitted across Phil's eyes, and she knew he was thinking about Ben. Fortunately, he made no mention of him. Instead, he said, "That's good to hear, Leah. I'm glad to see you."

Now she could feel Callie's eyes on her, and she

turned to find her daughter watching her intently, gaze swiveling from Leah to Phil and back again, expression hopeful. "It's good to see you too, Phil," she replied, though the words held no emotion. And very little truth.

Phil, sensing this, flinched and fell silent. An awkwardness settled over the two of them then, a silence that filled the air with thick, heavy tension that was only broken when Phil turned to Jeremy and engaged him in a conversation that lasted all the way through ordering their meals.

When their dinners finally arrived, Leah concentrated hard on her plate, and found herself daydreaming about Crystal Bay as a way to make it through the evening. She pictured her room at the inn, airy and bright, with million-dollar views that she'd spent hours admiring since she arrived. She imagined herself walking along the shore, sand in her toes, saltwater in her hair, the breeze warming her skin and the golden sun blazing down on her. She envisioned the seagulls soaring overhead, their wings tipped in sunshine, the dolphins leaping in and out of the waves, the sand crabs burrowing at her feet.

But most of all she thought of Ben, the way his honey eyes crinkled when he laughed, his whiskey voice that sent shivers down her spine, the feeling she had when she was with him that all was right in the world. A powerful wave of longing washed over her then, a need to see him, to talk to him, to simply be near him. Those old feelings were awakening— she knew this, she recognized it, but she had a hard time accepting it. The idea of being vulnerable again, the idea of opening herself up to the agony and beauty of love... it was too much to bear right now, when her wounds were still raw and her heart was still broken.

Thoughts of home carried her through dinner and dessert, made the evening bearable, and before she knew it, the bill was paid and everyone was gathering their things. As they stepped outside into the evening air, which was thick with the sounds of traffic and car horns rather than beach bonfires and crashing waves, they stood in a small group to say their goodbyes.

Andrew was the first to leave, offering his father a formal handshake before wrapping Leah in one final hug. "You going to be okay?" he whispered, pulling her away from the group. "I know tonight was hard for you."

"Not as hard as I expected." Leah cupped her son's cheek one last time. "And I promise, I'll be fine." She felt a hand on her arm and turned to find Callie behind her, expression inscrutable.

"Can I talk to you?" she asked, casting a glance at Phil and Jeremy, who were once more deep in conversation. "In private."

After saying their goodbyes to Andrew, she pulled Leah to the side of the restaurant, into the shadows. When they were alone, she took a deep breath and said, "That went well, don't you think?"

"Absolutely." Leah nodded toward Jeremy. "He's seems like a wonderful boy, Callie. I love him, and I can tell your father does too. I'm happy for you."

Callie shook her head. "That's not what I mean." She shifted nervously, heels clicking against concrete. "I mean you and Dad. You seemed... good."

"We're both trying our best," Leah answered cautiously. "No matter what happens between your father and me, we're still a family, and always will be. I want you to know that."

"No matter what happens?" Callie narrowed her eyes. "What's that supposed to mean?"

Leah was taken aback. "I'm not sure..."

"Mom, come on," Callie interrupted. "Isn't it time to end this whole... whatever *thing* it is you're doing?" She waved both hands in the air for emphasis. "I get that you're having some kind of mid-life crisis, but enough is enough. Dad misses you, and frankly, I think you're being selfish. You don't just walk out on your marriage because you're bored."

"Because I'm bored?" Leah echoed, incredulous. "Is that what you think happened?" She exhaled a steadying breath. "Believe it or not, Callie, there might be things going on between your father and me that you aren't privy to."

"Marriage is forever. It's a commitment. It's for *life*." Callie was near tears now; they were glistening on her eyelashes, highlighted by the streetlight's golden halo. "You don't get to just give up. I know Dad wanted you to go to counseling. I know he's been trying, and you're not."

Leah stared at her daughter for several long moments. Then, quietly, she said, "I think this conversation is over." She turned to leave, but her daughter stopped her with a hand on her arm.

"Please, Mom." Her voice was a gentle plea, and Leah felt her own tears blurring her vision. "Please don't give up on our family. Please don't give up on Dad. Please, just… come home."

Then she was gone, safely nestled between Jeremy and Phil as the three of them walked down the sidewalk to their respective cars, leaving Leah as the outsider once more.

"I HAVE AN IDEA."

Avery had waited until Molly left the inn for the evening before tracking down Danny, who was fixing a wobbly lamp in one of the guest rooms, sleeves rolled up to reveal his lithe, muscular arms.

"Is your idea that we finally buy a new one of these so I can stop tinkering with it every other day?" he asked, gesturing at the lamp in frustration. "I know it's one of your favorites, but seriously, Avery, I think I spend half of my work time trying to fix it."

"Not quite." Avery smiled at him, then produced a DVD from behind her back. "I was thinking... with your wedding coming up, you and Molly could probably use some ideas for the ceremony and reception. We had such a nice wedding, so I thought, why not take a look at our wedding video? See if it gets the gears turning?"

She sounded ridiculous, and she knew it. But desperate times called for desperate measures... and Avery was nothing if not desperate.

Danny squinted at her, scratched his chin with the base of his screwdriver. "You want to watch our wedding video?"

"Sure, why not? I haven't pulled it out in years." The truth was, Avery had watched it many times since the divorce—anytime she needed a good cry, that is, or a reminder of all they used to mean to each other. It helped assure her that what they had was real, that they were in love, despite what Danny may have believed.

He glanced at the clock on the wall, brow furrowed. "I wasn't planning on staying much longer. It's getting pretty late, and I'm sure Molly has gotten dinner started by now."

"Just for a few minutes." Avery held up the DVD once more. "Seriously, I think it'll be helpful. Molly told me she was having a hard time coming up with ideas for the ceremony—readings, songs, the whole bit. This will refresh your memory, give you some tips." She held her breath, waiting for him to respond.

Finally, after what seemed like an eternity, he shrugged. "If you say so. Sure... why not." Wiping the sweat from his brow, he followed her out of the room and down the steps to the parlor, where a television was anchored to the wall above the fireplace. Despite the balmy evening, Avery had decided that a fire was in order—and she had dimmed the lights, too, for an added ambience of romance.

Danny collapsed onto the couch as Avery popped in the DVD and grabbed the remote, and a few moments later, they were watching her walk down the aisle toward Danny, her face alight with the kind of happiness she hadn't felt since the day he walked out. "Look how young we were," she murmured as the camera panned to Danny, whose eyes were locked on Avery's, his expression one of pure devotion. "Look how happy."

"It was a good day," he agreed, propping one foot on the coffee table as he studied the screen. "I look ridiculous in my tux, though. Like a penguin."

"I think you look handsome."

He shot her a quick smile, then returned his attention to the television. "Oh, look, there's my grandmother," he said, leaning forward, elbows resting on his knees. "She looks so young there. I can't believe it's been so many years since she's passed."

"And my aunt," Avery murmured, eyes on the screen, on those who had joined in on the celebration of their love. "Remember she got us that ridiculous custom mailbox with the birds printed all over it? I still have it stored in the attic."

"Along with all the rest of the gifts we've never used," Danny added. "That's why Molly and I are requesting no gifts from our guests. We don't need anything, and they don't need to trouble themselves." He slid a glance toward Avery. "Molly said you'd agreed to read the poem at the ceremony. Thanks... that means a lot."

Avery was silent for several long moments, debating how to respond. Then, deciding to throw caution to the wind, she paused the video and turned to face him fully. "I have to ask, Danny... why that poem? Why *that* one? You know it had a special meaning for us."

He wrinkled his brow in confusion, a frown shadowing his mouth. Then, scratching his nails idly down the stubble on his cheeks, he said, "I'm not sure I know what you're referring to. Molly and I chose that poem because I happened to hear it many years ago and fell in love with it. It's symbolic of my relationship with her, of undying love."

By now, Avery was staring at him with a mix of disbelief and devastation. "Danny, you didn't *happen* to hear that poem many years ago. I introduced you to it. I used to recite it to you when..." She cleared her throat, swallowing back the tears threatening to form. "We used it in our ceremony. It's engraved on our *wedding* rings, for crying out loud. How can you not remember?"

To his credit, he looked mildly chagrined, but his tone was defensive as he said, "That was, like, twenty years ago, Avery. I barely remember what I had for breakfast, let alone what poem I heard when I was barely out of college."

"You had a bagel for breakfast," Avery snapped. "See? That wasn't so hard."

"Whoa." Danny held up his hands, palms out. "What's with the negativity? I thought we were enjoying a little blast from the past here." He gestured toward the video. "This was a long time ago, Avery. You can't fault me for not remembering every single thing about a wedding that ultimately ended in divorce."

Avery inhaled sharply, his words stinging her to the core. She opened her mouth to respond, then left it agape; she had no idea what to say. Danny was glaring at her now, and suddenly the video, the fire, the dim lighting… none of it seemed romantic in the least. It seemed suffocating. It seemed desperate.

Finally, she looked away from him, the tears still burning the back of her throat. She quietly switched on the video once more, and though their younger selves were still on the screen, holding hands and declaring their love for each other, Avery was no longer watching. Her eyes were unfocused, mind blank, heart shattered as completely as it had been five years ago, when this whole nightmare had started.

Danny, noticing her distress, slung an arm around her shoulders. "Sorry for being sore, Avery. I guess with the wedding coming up, and work being so busy, I'm just stressed. I want to watch the video with you—really, I do. It brings up some nice memories, and it's cool to see some of our family members again." He gestured toward the remote. "Here. Let's turn it up a little."

"That's okay." Avery's voice cracked, but she quickly recovered by offering him a wide smile. "No harm done. I actually just remembered that I forgot to get that load of towels started for room seven, so I'd better go do that." She paused. "See you tomorrow?"

"You betcha." Danny stood and stretched while Avery busied herself with tidying up a few magazines strewn around the parlor. When she looked up next, Danny was gone, and a moment later she heard the distant sound of the front door shutting.

Finally allowing herself to break down, she slumped onto the couch, head resting against the cushion, tears streaming freely down her cheeks and soaking into her shirt. She reached for the remote and pressed play, then wept as she silently mouthed the words to the vows she knew by heart as her younger self did the same on the screen. A few minutes later the ceremony ended and the reception began, and she watched through bleary eyes as she and Danny swayed in each other's arms for their first dance, smeared each other's faces with wedding cake, and then, laughing, kissed it off.

The camera had just panned to a close-up of their faces when Avery heard footsteps approaching. Straightening up and wiping the tears from her cheeks, she paused the video just as Max Wallace rounded the corner into the parlor, humming to himself, trusty laptop tucked under his arm.

Seeing her, he stopped short, eyes swiveling from the fireplace, to the screen, to the pile of tissues on her lap. "I'm sorry," he said, backtracking a few steps. "I didn't mean to interrupt."

"You're not interrupting anything." She leaned across the couch to switch on the lamp, bathing the room in a soft yellow glow. "Come on in."

He hesitated, then stepped inside, perching on the far end of the couch and cocking his head in curiosity. "What's that?" he asked, gesturing to the screen, where she and Danny were frozen mid-laugh. He squinted. "Is that you, and the other guy who runs this place?"

"It is indeed." Avery heaved a sigh. "It's my wedding video. I wish I could say I was just taking a trip down memory lane, but it's a lot more pathetic than that."

"Trust me, I know pathetic." Max set his laptop on the coffee table and settled himself more comfortably against the cushions, eyes intent as they studied her face. "Want to talk about it?"

"Not really." Then she glanced at him, and something about the expression on his face—kind, warm, *interested*—caused her to break. "You see, I'm sort of... I'm sort of in love with my ex-husband. Who just so happens to be getting married again in a couple of months. And I'm trying to win him back." She winced. "Pretty bad, huh?"

"Not great." Max gave her a soft smile. "Not the worst I've heard either."

Avery laughed. "I guess I'll take some comfort in that."

They were quiet for a time after that, both watching the flames flickering in the hearth, both listening to the crackling of the logs and the distant sound of the waves lapping against the shoreline. Then, shifting on the couch to face her, he said,

"How's this for pathetic? I thought my wife loved me, but I'm pretty sure she only married me for my money. It took me years to admit that to myself, and even now, it's painful."

"How sad, for both of you," Avery murmured. Noting his use of the past tense when referring to his wife, and reading the hurt in his eyes, she said, "Are the two of you...?"

"Separated," Max supplied, "although no one knows but the two of us, and now you. She wants to keep up appearances, and I've decided it's easier for me just to go along with it."

"I watched her. On *Society Wives*? She was... something." Avery raised her eyebrows at him, a smile curling her lips. "She made quite the impression."

"And now you know why we're separated." He let out a laugh that was edged in bitterness. "When she started on the show, she created this... persona. This character. And then the more she got immersed in that world, the more the character became a part of her. By the time we decided to end things, I couldn't tell one from the other anymore. The woman I married no longer exists."

"I'm sorry." There was nothing else for her to say, no other words of comfort to offer him.

A pause, then, "I'm sorry too. For you. Your situation can't be easy."

She shrugged, then the two of them lapsed into silence again. Even though they weren't speaking, his presence was solid and reassuring, a comfort to her despite the fact that they were virtual strangers. Eventually, with a glance at his laptop, she asked, "How's the writing coming? Has being in Crystal Bay helped inspiration strike?"

"Believe it or not, it has." Max perked up noticeably. "I've written more this past week than I have over the last year. And it's not total garbage, either." He cringed. "At least I hope it's not. My agent will be the final judge of that."

Gazing out the window at the dusky purple sky highlighted by the last rays of the dying sun, he said, "This really is a beautiful place. I couldn't stand living in Manhattan any longer. The traffic, the crowds, the lifestyle... I'm not cut out for any of it. I actually grew up in a small town, too. Thought I'd stay there my whole life. Then things took off with my writing, and I found myself traveling to New York all the time, so eventually I decided it would be easier just to move there. A few months later I met Vanessa, and I guess the rest is history." He shrugged. "You can move the boy into the city, but you can never move the city into the boy. Towns like this are in my blood."

Then, glancing at the grandfather clock in the corner, he said, "I'd better be heading back to my room. I'm hoping to fit in another chapter before hitting the sack for the night." He smiled at her, eyes sparkling in the dim light. "Thanks for the company and the conversation. I enjoyed myself, despite the subject matter."

"I did too." Avery tipped her chin up to meet his gaze, then raised her hand in a goodbye wave. As he started to leave, she said, "Oh! I forgot to mention. I received a strange phone call here the other day—a news reporter, looking for you. I didn't give her any information, though. Any idea what that was about?"

He looked unbothered by the news. "Someone probably got wind that I was in town and wanted to set up an interview. Even though I'm a has-been, it still happens from time to time. The last thing I want while I'm here is any attention, especially from the media, so thanks for covering for me. I appreciate it."

"No problem." Avery stood to draw the curtains after one last glance at the indigo sea. "I'll see you around, okay?" She offered him a shy smile. "Good-night, Max."

He tipped his head in her direction. "Goodnight, Avery."

She waited for him to leave, listening to his footsteps creaking up the staircase and along the upstairs hallway before hearing his door shut with a distant *thud*. Only then did she sink back onto the couch in the darkness and lose herself in her own grief once more.

CHAPTER 9

*A*s the weathered, slightly crooked sign for Crystal Bay came into view, a lightness settled over Leah, a feeling that all was right in her world once more. Pulling into the inn's parking lot brought with it a sense of profound relief, and the first thing she did upon exiting her car was to walk directly onto the beach, sinking her toes into the sand and enjoying the salty breeze playing across her skin.

"It's good to be back," she whispered to herself as a nearby seagull watched her curiously, orange eyes blazing. "I have nothing for you," she added to the bird with a laugh, showing it her empty pockets.

The seagull, after tossing her a look of deep disgust, took flight, its white wings shimmering against the crystalline sky. She watched it soar over the sea, reveling in the sun-soaked day, the single puffy cloud that floated high above the waves, the sounds of children laughing and splashing in the water nearby. Spending time in the city—and with Phil—had allowed her to appreciate her hometown in an entirely new way, allowed her to see its beauty and charm with fresh eyes and an open heart. She'd cut her trip short by half a day, opting to pack up and leave her hotel as soon as the first rays of dawn broke through the hazy early-morning sky.

The previous night had been emotionally draining, and even though she'd tried to reach out to Callie, her daughter had thus far remained stubbornly silent. It left a hole in Leah's already battered heart, even more so when she considered that eventually she would have to tell Callie the truth, and ruin her little girl's belief in Phil's status as a superhero, quite possibly forever. Even though she had no intentions of bad-mouthing her husband to their children, the fact remained that Callie now had two brothers—and deserved to know the truth.

But right now, she had to table the prospect of that conversation because she had an equally pressing one to attend to. With an anxious glance behind her at the inn, and a longing one at the ocean in front of her, she turned and began traipsing through the sand, her thoughts on Remi and everything she had told her about Avery's plans on winning Danny back.

No, scratch that. Her plans on ripping Molly out of Danny's arms, permanently.

It was crazy. It was bound to fail. It was also unbearably, gut-wrenchingly sad.

Leah had no illusions that she could stop her. But she at least wanted to offer an ear to listen or, if necessary, a shoulder to cry on. Avery would do the same for her in a heartbeat.

Pushing open the inn's front door, and steeling herself for the unpleasant conversation awaiting her, Leah was surprised to see Avery behind the desk, laughing as she gazed up at none other than Max Wallace, annoying guest extraordinaire. He was leaning against the opposite side of the desk, graying hair casually tousled, stunningly blue eyes sparkling with amusement. Leah found herself automatically admiring him—with his movie-star good looks, it was hard not to. But the scene confused her; the last time she checked, Avery was ready to throw Max right out the window. Preferably one of the *upper-story* windows.

"Leah, you're back!" There was a musical lilt to

Avery's voice that Leah hadn't heard in a long time. "How was your trip?" Turning to Max, she added, "If you're looking for a harrowing story, ask Leah to tell you about her marriage sometime." At Leah's look of surprise bordering on shock, she laughed and gestured between herself and Max. "We've been comparing horror stories about our love life. Apparently we're both in the running for worst relationship of all time."

"Somehow I think I have you both beat." She turned to Max, hand extended. "Hi, I'm Leah. My husband of twenty-five years fathered a child with my best friend thirteen years ago and I only found out last month."

Max's mouth dropped open almost comically. "Okay, you win," he said, throwing up his hands in defeat. "*That* is the worst relationship story I've ever heard."

"Yeah, well, I always did like to win." Leah smirked. "Nice to meet you, Max. I'm a big fan of your book—I've read it at least three times."

Max inclined his head graciously, then gestured to his laptop. "And speaking of that, I'd better get to work. Thanks for the company, Avery. It's always a pleasure. Leah, it was nice to meet you too. I'm sure I'll be seeing you around." With a final nod at both women, he strode out to the porch, settling himself in one of the Adirondack chairs overlooking the water.

When he was safely out of earshot, Leah turned to her sister, eyebrows raised. "What was *that* about? I thought you couldn't stand him."

"I never said I couldn't stand him. I said he was a terrible customer. But we've come to an understanding recently. He's actually a really nice guy."

"Is he now?" Leah's eyebrows ticked up even further, but Avery shot down her silent question with a firm shake of her head.

"Whatever you're thinking, get it out of your head. The man is married. Well, separated, but still. No."

"Which brings me to my next topic of conversation." Leah grabbed a nearby armchair and dragged it over to the desk, glancing over her shoulder to ensure that Danny was nowhere in sight. "I had an... interesting... conversation with Remi before I left. She's worried about you. About some things you've said to her recently."

Avery looked momentarily outraged, and then her shoulders slumped. Turning back to the computer, she said, "The last thing I need right now is a lecture."

"And I'm not trying to give you one." Leah leaned forward and switched off the screen, forcing her sister to look at her. "I'm trying to stop you from doing something you'll regret."

Avery laughed hollowly. "Don't you get it? I have no time for regrets. This is my last chance, Leah. It's my last chance to make him understand, to make him realize that what we had... it was real, and perfect, and wonderful."

"Not to him it wasn't." Leah's voice was gentle but firm despite the devastation that flashed across Avery's face at her words. But she had no other choice—Avery needed to accept reality, not live in the past. The worst thing, the absolute *worst* thing, she needed right now was false hope. And Leah had no plans of giving her any.

"I'm not trying to hurt you, Avery—please understand that." Leah took her sister's hand, which was shaking. Avery immediately pulled away, crossing her arms over her body, warding off Leah's words. "But Danny has had five years to change his mind, and he hasn't. We can't force other people to love us, Avery. No matter how painful that is, it's the truth. Danny and Molly are getting married, and no amount of trying to come between them is going to make a difference. I don't want to see you embarrass yourself. I don't want to see you any more hurt than you already are."

"You don't know what you're talking about." Two spots of color had appeared high on Avery's cheeks. "And moreover, you're wrong. Dead wrong."

"I'm not wrong." Leah wanted to grab her sister by the shoulders and shake some sense into her. But she also knew that grief did funny things to a person, and right now, she wasn't talking to Avery. She was talking to Avery's broken heart. "Avery, can't you just—"

"I don't have time for this right now, Leah." Avery was on her feet and gathering a pen and notebook as she glanced at the clock. "I have a meeting to get to."

"A… meeting?" Leah stared at her in confusion. "You don't have any staff here except you and Danny. What kind of meeting could you possibly be going to?"

Avery averted her eyes, though her cheeks were flushed pink. "If you must know, I have a meeting with Danny and Molly. To discuss their engagement party, which they're holding here at the inn tomorrow night. And before you try and stop me," she added, holding up a hand to cut off Leah, who had opened her mouth in horror at this new development, "it's fine. Everything is fine. Just… leave me alone, okay? I can make my own decisions." She hesitated. "And if this whole thing ends poorly, at least I can go to sleep at night knowing I tried. Sometimes the chances we don't take define the rest of our life, and Leah... like everyone else, yourself included, I just want to be happy."

Leah studied her sister's face, the sadness etched in every one of her beautiful features. Then, quietly, she nodded. For what else was there to say? At the end of the day, both sisters wanted the same thing: peace, and a heart that was fully mended.

And only time would tell if either one of them would get it.

MAYBE IT WAS the conversation she had with her sister, or maybe it was the knowledge, deep within her bones, that she needed to explore the feelings she'd been suppressing for so many years, but later that evening, Leah found herself standing outside The Beach Bum, heart in her throat as she listened to the buzz of conversation floating out from the bar. Ben was in there somewhere, maybe thinking of her, maybe wondering if she would return or decide to remain with Phil.

She hadn't contacted him yet; she'd needed time to think, to get her plans in order.

Or plan, she supposed she should say, because there was only one. To stay in Crystal Bay, to make a life for herself in the place that perhaps she never should have left in the first place—and with the man she never should have left behind.

Would things work out between them? Could their friendship truly blossom into what they had both secretly wanted for so long? Only time would tell... but in order for that to happen, Leah had to allow them to take the first step.

The bar's familiar musty smell greeted her as she pushed open the door and peered around the dimly lit interior, her eyes seeking out Ben. She found him in his usual spot behind the bar, shaker in one hand, martini glass in the other, laughing along with a group of thirty-something women in revealing outfits who were crowded around the bar, openly flirting with him. Leah felt a stab of jealousy at the sight of them—she could never compete with women like that, just like, at the end of the day, she hadn't been able to compete with Kate.

Then Ben's eyes met hers across the room, and time stopped.

"Hey there," she said, weaving her way through

the women and slipping onto the bar stool across from him.

"Hey yourself." He smiled at her, though she could see the caution in his eyes, the question lingering behind his smile.

"I'm back," she said, vaguely aware that the group of women had moved away from them, looking disappointed.

"You're back." Ben leaned his elbows against the bar, gaze probing as it settled on her face.

"Yes, I'm back. And I was wondering…" Leah shifted uneasily in her seat as the nerves set in. Taking a deep breath, she continued, "I was wondering if you'd like to have dinner with me tomorrow night. *Not* as friends."

At this, Ben's face split into a grin. "I would love nothing more. Pick you up at seven?"

"No." Leah's grin matched his own. "I'll pick *you* up at seven."

CHAPTER 10

"*H*ave you looked out the window recently?" Leah was peering through the curtains on the inn's picture window the following morning, her back to Avery, while the latter organized the pair of reservations that had come in overnight.

"No, why?" Avery asked in a vague voice, eyes on the screen. "Did I tell you we have a full house again next week? We usually aren't this busy until summertime is in full swing. Danny set us up on one of those traveler review sites—I bet it's from that." Then, when Leah didn't answer, she glanced up to find her sister's nose still pressed to the window. "Why are you standing there like that? Does it look like it's going to rain?"

"No, it looks like there's about a dozen news vans congregating in your parking lot, and three more circling the inn, trying to find a place to park."

"What?" Avery jumped to her feet and joined her sister at the window. Sure enough, a crowd of news reporters and cameramen were in the process of setting up their equipment in the parking lot, many of them using the inn as their backdrop. She turned to her sister, wide-eyed. "What do you think they want?"

"Did you murder someone?" Leah asked, eyes equally wide as she shifted to the side of the window so no one would see her. "Or rob a bank?"

"I'm pretty sure I spent the night in my own bed, sleeping." Then, remembering the telephone call, she gasped. "They must be here for Max!"

"For *Max*?" Leah whipped the curtains over the window when one of the reporters spotted her and began pointing. "What did he do?"

"I have no idea. I mentioned to him that a reporter called the inn looking for him the other day, and he didn't seem to think it was a big deal. He figured someone must have gotten wind that he was in town and wanted an interview, said it still happened from time to time." She glanced at the grandfather clock, noting that it was nearly nine a.m.

"I'm sure he's awake by now. I'd better knock on his door." Pointing to the front door, she added, "Do *not* open it for anyone. I don't want to spook the rest of my guests."

"I'm pretty sure they'll be spooked just by looking out their windows, but I'll do my best to hold down the fort." Leah inched away from the window as another pair of news vans arrived and crammed themselves into the parking lot. She sank into the chair that Avery had previously occupied and pulled up a blank tab on the Internet. "I'll do a quick Google search and see if I can find any information."

In the meantime, Avery was halfway up the steps, mind racing as she tried to figure out what was going on. Her inn had never attracted any kind of attention before, outside of the initial article that had appeared in the local paper after she and Danny had completed their renovations. Seeing all of those reporters unnerved her, so she couldn't even begin to imagine what the rest of Crystal Bay was thinking.

Probably that she had gotten herself into something illegal. Or dangerous.

Great. This was just what she needed right now, on top of everything else.

Annoyed, she banged on Max's door, then stood

back, arms crossed tightly as she waited for him to answer. "Coming," he called, then she heard the distant sound of the bathroom sink turn on before he appeared a minute later, towel in his hands, hair still dripping from a recent bath. When he saw her mutinous expression, he frowned. "Was it something I said?"

"Or something you *did*." She scowled at him. "This is a quaint, quiet inn, and I'd like to keep it that way."

He nodded slowly, still looking perplexed. "That's understandable."

She threw up her hands in frustration. "Why, then, are there about twenty news vans circling my inn like piranhas?" Glaring at him, she added, "They must be here for you."

"For *me*?" Max looked taken aback. Leaving the door to his room open, he strode to the window, pulling back the curtains to peer out, Avery hot on his heels. He studied the scene outside with interest for a few moments, then turned back to Avery, frowning once more. "I don't get it. Why would you think they're here for me?"

"Because of that phone call I got the other day. The reporter, asking if you were staying here?" She pressed her hands to her hips. "I don't know about you, but this doesn't look like someone simply wants to interview you. This looks a whole lot more serious than that, and the last thing my inn needs is negative attention."

"Give me a few minutes to get ready and I'll go outside and get this sorted out." Max began pulling open drawers and haphazardly grabbing items of clothing before yanking his current shirt over his head to reveal a smooth, tan stomach.

Avery, cheeks reddening, quickly averted her eyes, then headed for the door. "I'll go out with you," she called over her shoulder, pulling the door closed behind her. "When you're ready, meet me at the front desk."

When she bounded back down the stairs, she could hear the inn's phone ringing, followed by a cautious "Hello?" from Leah, who was still manning the desk. "No, I'm sorry, I don't know what you're referring to," she was saying as Avery jogged toward the desk, motioning to the phone.

When Leah passed it to her, she issued a curt, "No comment," before hanging up. Then, thinking better of it, she switched the phone off altogether, hoping that no reservation requests came in over the next few minutes. Right now, she needed to focus on sorting out the circus happening outside her

157

window—and sending the reporters away as soon as possible.

"I'm here," Max said a minute later, jogging down the stairs, slightly breathless. He headed directly for the front door as Avery fell into step beside him. When they emerged onto the inn's porch, every head swung their way, and after a beat, a swarm of reporters rushed toward them, microphones at the ready, shouting questions at him that jumbled together in the commotion.

Max, for his part, remained unruffled, holding up his hands and saying, "One at a time, folks, please. I have no idea what's going on right now, and shouting questions at me isn't going to get me to answer them any faster."

A middle-aged blonde reporter shoved herself through the crowd until she reached the porch steps, then raised her microphone toward Max and said, "What comments do you have for our viewers on your wife's arrest?"

Avery's eyes widened and her head swiveled toward Max, who was standing frozen in place, a look of complete shock on his face. There was silence for a few moments before he said, his voice heavy with disbelief, "What did you say? My wife's... *arrest*?"

"Surely you've heard about it by now." The blonde glanced at the reporters to her left and right, who were both scribbling furiously in their notebooks. "Your wife Vanessa was arrested late last night for fraud. Her charity, the New York City Childhood Leukemia Foundation, has been under federal investigation for some time. According to the arrest warrant, she has been diverting funds received from donors into an offshore bank account." She raised one neatly penciled eyebrow at him. "Are you going on record saying that you know nothing about this?"

"I know nothing about this." Max's voice was clear and strong, but Avery could see that his hands were trembling. "As far as I am aware, Vanessa's charity has been successfully raising funds and donating them to cancer research for the past three years. Any other activities are completely outside of my awareness. And..." He hesitated, then pressed on, "Vanessa and I have been separated for a year and a half now. During that time, we have had very little contact, which would explain why I have no knowledge of her arrest."

"Mr. Wallace, are you aware that you are listed on the board of directors for the foundation?" a young man in a pressed suit and polished shoes asked, stepping up beside the blonde. "You've been heavily featured in photos taken at various charity events held in Manhattan to benefit the foundation, oftentimes appearing alongside your wife, many of them over the past year. Now you're claiming that you're separated?"

"We've maintained a business relationship, and that's it." Max's hands had curled into fists at his side, and Avery took an automatic step toward him, a protective step, though she had no idea why. She supposed it was because he looked so vulnerable right now. His hair was mussed from the shower, his clothes were mismatched, and he wasn't even wearing shoes. She could only imagine the headlines that would pop up in newspapers and gossip websites around the country tomorrow.

With that in mind, Avery stepped forward, positioning herself in front of Max to block him from the cameras that were now beginning to flash all around them. "Mr. Wallace isn't taking any more questions at this time. Furthermore, this is private property, and I have to ask you to leave. If you don't pack up and leave the premises in the next ten minutes, I'm going to call the police."

Then she grabbed a still-stunned Max by the arm

and marched him back inside the inn while, behind them, the reporters continued shouting questions into the air. When they were safely inside, Avery slammed the door, then yanked the blinds down over the windows to block them from view. Most of the reporters were trickling back to their vans, though a few of them were still milling around the inn's property, no doubt hoping for a chance to ask more questions. Seeing this, Avery slipped her cell phone out of her pocket and set a timer for ten minutes—she'd meant every word she said about calling the police.

Then, glancing around for the first time, she groaned softly when she saw Leah gathered in the inn's parlor with a cluster of her other guests, trying to calm them down as they peered out the window with a mix of curiosity and fear. Setting down her phone, she headed into the parlor to reassure them that everything was all right and gave a quick explanation of what had happened, without mentioning Max by name, before issuing each of them vouchers for a free weekend stay to compensate them for their troubles.

They left the parlor looking noticeably happier, with Avery trailing behind them, mentally calculating just how much money this little scene had cost her. Max, hearing all of this, was still standing by the desk with a look of chagrin.

"I'm so sorry about all of this," he said, raking both hands through his hair until it stood on end. "Please believe me when I say that I'm as shocked as you are right now. I..." He swallowed hard. "I can't believe what I'm hearing, but it must be true. Vanessa, *arrested?*" He shook his head. "She put so much into that charity, gave so much of her time. There must be some kind of mistake."

Avery gave him a sympathetic smile, any lingering annoyance melting away when she saw how helpless he looked right then. "You had no idea this was happening?"

"Not a clue. *If* it's happening," he clarified. "I was involved in the charity in name only—this was Vanessa's baby, and has been from the start." He ran his hands down his cheeks, then cupped them over his mouth, his blue eyes saturated with confusion. "Vanessa isn't a saint, I'll be the first to admit that— but *stealing*? From a children's charity?" He was shaking his head again, this time harder. "I refuse to believe that."

"It could be a mistake," Leah interjected gently. "Remember, an arrest doesn't mean a conviction. Your wife is innocent until proven guilty."

"Except in the court of public opinion." Max sighed, suddenly looking bone-weary. "If she did this, if she *did* this…" He swallowed hard. "Then she didn't just ruin herself. She ruined me too."

"I HEAR you had quite the morning."

Danny appeared quite unexpectedly in the kitchen, where Avery was savoring a mug of tea and trying to steel herself for the evening ahead. Once again, Leah thought she was crazy, this time for agreeing to host—and help organize—Danny and Molly's engagement party at the inn. And once again, Avery privately agreed with her, while outwardly resenting her sister's intrusion.

"It was a zoo." She smiled at him over the rim of her mug, then gestured to the table. "Would you like to join me?"

"Don't mind if I do." Danny helped himself to a mug of tea, then sank into the seat opposite her with a sigh. "I could use a break. Things have been crazy lately." He leaned back in his chair, and under the bright kitchen lights, Avery could see the lines of exhaustion around his eyes. "Sometimes I think running this inn is too much for me—it's too constant. There's so little opportunity to even take a vacation, and when I do, I feel guilty for leaving everything in your hands."

He took a long sip of his tea, savoring it, eyes closed. Then, opening them, he said, "I suppose having Molly on board will help with the workload."

"It's definitely more than a full-time job for each of us," Avery murmured, watching the steam spiral from her mug and dissipate in the air. Voice turning nostalgic, she said, "Do you remember the day we got the keys to this place? We were so excited."

"And terrified," Danny added, chuckling. "Since we knew exactly nothing about owning and operating any kind of business, let alone one as complex as an inn."

"We had a dream, and we followed through with it." Avery, on instinct, reached across the table and covered his hand with hers. "And look how much we've accomplished since then. I'm proud of us."

Danny gazed silently, contemplatively, down at her hand for a long moment. When he glanced up, she was startled to see tears in his eyes. "I owe you an apology," he said, squeezing her hand, and then holding on to it tightly. "These past few weeks, for whatever reason, I've started thinking a lot about the past. Our past." He swallowed hard, Adam's apple bobbing, while Avery sat frozen across from him, heart in her throat, barely daring to breathe.

His eyes now locked on hers, he whispered, "We were good together, weren't we."

"We were great." Avery's own eyes filled with tears that began spilling down her cheeks, but for the first time in his presence, she made no move to wipe them away. "We were so great."

He leaned across the table to pat away her tears with the pads of his fingers, then allowed his hand to linger there, caressing her skin, while she let her eyes drift closed against his touch, the feeling she'd craved and been denied for so long. "Why did you do it?" she asked as the hot tears continued to flow. "Why did you walk away?"

"Because I was young, and stupid, and scared." He inhaled shakily, then let the breath out on a soft sigh. "At that time, we had so much responsibility. The inn was taking up all of our time, we barely had a relationship outside of our business meetings, and then we were talking about adding kids to the mix..." He shook his head. "It was all too much for me. I couldn't handle it, so I just... bolted." He gave her hand a gentle squeeze. "In hindsight, I did the wrong thing. And I'm sorry, Avery. Truly, I am."

"I'm sorry too," she whispered, though in truth,

she had no idea why she was apologizing. "Maybe I could have paid more attention to you, been more in tune with your needs…" She swallowed hard, glanced away. "I never stopped loving you, you know."

Danny's eyes were impossibly bright as he tipped her face back toward him with his finger. "I never stopped loving you, either. It's taken me far too long to realize that."

The room drained of air then, leaving Avery with only the rapid beating of her heart, only the sound of Danny scraping back his chair and pulling her up into his arms. He caressed her face once more, his touch whisper-light, as though he feared she would break. Then he cupped her cheeks in his warm hands, and when their lips touched, her knees felt weak and she knew, right then, that she was in heaven.

CHAPTER 11

"What are you so happy about?"

Leah shot her sister a suspicious look as she passed the front desk to find her whistling yet again. Avery had been practically floating around the inn all afternoon, despite the flurry of preparations happening for Danny and Molly's engagement party, which would take place outside on the sand in a few hours. The caterer had already arrived and was preparing a sumptuous dinner in the kitchen, the rental company was currently setting up cocktail tables and seating areas in the sand, and the bartender was lining up all the ingredients he needed for the specialty drink that Molly had concocted to commemorate the occasion.

Yet Avery seemed to notice none of this. Instead, she just kept... whistling.

In denial, probably.

Leah furrowed her brow in her sister's direction. "Are you okay?"

"I'm awesome," Avery practically sing-songed. She gestured out the window. "Isn't it a gorgeous day? I was thinking later tonight you and I could build a fire on the beach, like old times. You know, enjoy a couple glasses of wine, some girl talk. Oh! We could even invite Mom."

Leah stared at Avery in alarm. "Invite *Mom*? Now I *know* something's wrong." She sidled up to her sister and attempted to place a palm on her forehead to check for a fever—and whatever delusions it was currently bringing on—but Avery batted her hand away with a laugh.

"Sure, why not? You know she's dying to spend more time with us." Then, switching from whistling to humming a cheerful tune, she glanced at the grandfather clock and said, "Look at the time! I'd better get ready for tonight." She gave Leah a bright smile. "Do you want to come to the party? I'm sure Danny won't mind."

"The party?" Leah cocked her head in confusion at her sister's almost gleeful tone. "You mean the engagement party." She said the words slowly, carefully, as if she were speaking to a particularly dimwitted toddler. "Danny and Molly's *engagement* party."

"Yep, that's the one!" Avery had pulled out a bottle of nail polish from the desk drawer and was adding a coat of shimmering pink to her nails. "You can be my plus-one."

"Actually, I have a date tonight. With Ben." Leah could scarcely believe the words she was saying, so unbelievable were they after the many years spent daydreaming about this night. She felt seventeen again, when she was head over heels in love with the boy next door, hoping he would finally stop seeing her as a friend and open his eyes to the possibility of something much, much more.

Now that day was here. And she was terrified, and excited, and hopeful. Above all, in the midst of all the heartbreak she'd recently endured, she was hopeful.

"Oh, Leah, that's wonderful. That's absolutely wonderful. And also, I knew this day would come." Avery gave her sister a sly smile. "Once you returned to Crystal Bay, it was only a matter of time. True love can't be denied, you know. It always has a way of making itself known."

Something in the tone of Avery's voice—a dreamy quality Leah hadn't heard in years, and only when her sister was referring to Danny—gave Leah pause. Rapping her knuckles on the desk to get Avery's attention, she waited for her to look up from polishing her nails and said, "What's going on, Avery? You're not planning to... do something at the party tonight, are you?"

Avery raised a skeptical eyebrow. "'Do something?' What could I possibly be planning to do?" She began blowing on her nails to dry them. "I'm just in a good mood, that's all. Would you be happier if I was wailing and tearing my hair out, Leah? Would that be a more appropriate mood?"

"No, of course not," Leah muttered, feeling suitably chagrined. "I'm just..." She trailed off, then shrugged. "I'm glad you're in a good mood. And thanks for the invite to the party, but I'll be heading out to meet Ben before it starts. Maybe I'll take you up on that offer of a beach bonfire, though." She stepped back from the desk. "I'll leave you to it, okay?"

"Okay."

Avery barely spared a glance in her direction, leaving Leah with no option but to return to her room to begin preparing for the evening. Ben had offered to cook for the two of them at his place, but Leah had gently shot down that idea—she wasn't ready for the intimacy that implied, especially now, when she was still so vulnerable.

Instead, she wanted the two of them to start slow, get to know each other in this whole new way and see where it took them. Leah had no illusions that things were destined to work out—her marriage to Phil had taught her that—but the possibility of a different kind of future, the kind she had spent so many of her younger years envisioning, brought about a kind of breathless anticipation she'd never experienced before.

She was crazy about Ben. It had just taken her more than forty years to do something about it.

Still, part of her felt guilty, like she was doing something wrong, betraying Phil in some fundamental way. Which was ridiculous, she knew, since he was the one who ultimately torpedoed their marriage. If he hadn't betrayed her so deeply, the two of them would still be together, and her feelings for Ben would have remained right where they were for the past four decades: a golden memory of her youth, precious and sacred, something to be stored under lock and key and examined only when a particularly powerful wave of nostalgia struck her.

Her cell phone rang then, and she picked it up with no small measure of trepidation, fearing that it would be Phil, there to put a damper on her evening, there to make her question whether her choices were born out of hope or desperation. But it wasn't Phil, it was her mother... and Leah wasn't sure which prospect was worse.

"Hey, Mom," she answered with practiced cheerfulness. "How are you?"

"I'm fine, dear. I was just calling to see how you were doing. I felt bad about our little..." She paused. "...disagreement, the other night."

Leah frowned into the phone, wondering whether her ears were deceiving her. Cynthia Hart didn't do apologies, and this was the closest to an apology she was going to get. "I'm good, Mom, thanks for calling." She hesitated. The last thing she wanted was another "disagreement" when she told her mother about her date with Ben, but Crystal Bay's gossip mill was a well-oiled machine, and she knew Cynthia would find out about it sooner rather than later. Better to rip off the bandage now.

"Ben and I are seeing each other tonight."

A very pregnant pause, followed by, "I see. Is that wise?"

"It is." Leah's tone was no-nonsense. "I know you

think I'm making a mistake, but I saw Phil over the weekend, and I felt nothing. Absolutely nothing. In fact, I wanted to get as far away from him as I could, as quickly as I could."

Her mother's sigh was long-suffering. "Marriage takes work, Leah. You can't just wave a magic wand and expect everything to be fixed in an instant." Then, after another long pause, she said, "Perhaps it would be good for you to have your fun with Ben. Goodness knows you've been mooning after him since you were a child. And then, once you've had your fill, you and Phil can give things another try."

Leah opened her mouth hotly to respond, and then closed it again. Arguing was pointless. Trying to reason with the woman was pointless. Instead, she said, "Thanks for the advice. I have to get going, okay? I'll catch up with you later."

"Bye, dear," her mother said. "When you're out with Ben tonight, just keep in mind that you're still a married woman. We don't want people talking." She hung up without another word, leaving Leah holding the phone, fuming as she stared down at the blank screen.

Then she heard a knock at her door, and shook off her anger as she padded across the room to answer it. Avery was on the other side, grinning at her from behind a dozen of the most beautiful coral roses Leah had ever seen.

"Special delivery," her sister announced, passing the bouquet to Leah. "From a *very* special someone." Leaning forward, she closed the door to Leah's room, leaving her standing just inside the threshold, admiring the bouquet's delicate scent and reaching for the note tucked inside.

It was a plain white card with a simple message, the handwriting as familiar to her as her own.

Looking forward to tonight, and many nights to come.

"So am I," she murmured, brushing her fingertips against Ben's writing, caressing each letter he had written, each word that came from the heart. "So am I."

"Wow, Leah, you look... you look beautiful."

Ben's eyes swept over her as she approached him in the restaurant where they'd agreed to meet. She hadn't expected her nerves to be quite so all-consuming, and on the short drive to the restaurant, she'd had to give herself multiple pep talks just to pluck up the courage to step out of the car and hand her keys to the valet.

It's just Ben, she'd reminded herself at least a dozen times.

But that was the point—it was *Ben.* Her Ben, as she used to think of him. As a girl, she'd dreamed of this day more times than she could count, and now that it was here… she was absolutely terrified.

Seeing him now put her at ease, though, reminded her that he was still the boy she'd always known, and she stood on tiptoe to press a soft kiss to his cheek. "You look great too," she said, doing a double take at the sight of him in a gray blazer, dark-wash jeans, and a plum-colored button-down shirt. It was a far cry from his usual uniform of old T-shirt, baggy khakis, and flip-flops—when he wasn't barefoot—and the effect was… nice.

Very nice.

"Shall we?" he asked, offering her his arm. "Our table awaits."

She tucked her arm in his and together they walked through the dimly lit restaurant, which was filled with the sounds of soft conversation and clinking silverware. A violinist was strolling among the tables, playing beautiful melodies that lifted into the air; seeing this, Leah gave Ben a gentle nudge in the side. "You didn't have to choose something so fancy. I would have been happy grabbing a burger."

Despite her original plans, he had insisted on organizing the date, and it hadn't taken much convincing for her to acquiesce.

He smiled at her, his honey-brown eyes twinkling in the candlelight. "I wanted tonight to be perfect." They stopped beside a table near the window, which offered spectacular views of the sun slipping beneath the horizon, painting the darkening sea in hues of coral and gold that could never be replicated on paper. The table itself was decorated with a white cloth and tea candles, and another stunning bouquet of roses was arranged across one of the plates.

Ben carefully lifted the roses and pressed them into Leah's arms. "For you," he murmured, before helping her into her chair. She spent a few moments admiring the scenery, then turned her attention to Ben, who was now seated opposite her and gazing at her with the type of longing she immediately recognized, because once upon a time, in the not-so-distant past, she'd looked at him the same way.

"So," she said, smiling at him over the rim of her water glass. "Here we are."

"Here we are," he agreed. He reached one hand across the table, palm up, an invitation that she immediately accepted. She placed her hand in his, and he gave her fingers a soft squeeze. "I'm not going to dance around the subject, Leah. I've been waiting —hoping—for this night to happen for a long, long time." His eyes darkened as they met hers, and a shiver rolled down her spine. Then he smiled at her and picked up his menu, though he continued holding her hand, leaving her with a dry mouth and a racing heart and a feeling that this—all of it—was so, so right.

Ben's hand remained in hers as they ordered drinks and dinner, listened to the violinist when he stopped by their table, and made small talk about their days. As the evening progressed, Leah felt herself relaxing, felt her nerves melting away, and before long, they had slipped back into the easy conversation and playful banter they had always enjoyed.

Before she knew it, they had cleaned their plates and were lingering over dessert, and Ben had shifted his chair so that they were now sitting beside each other, so close their arms kept brushing, sending more tingles of electricity racing over Leah's skin. On more than one occasion she was positive that Ben was going to kiss her, and even though his gaze kept wandering to her lips, lingering there, he made no move to draw her into his arms.

They left the restaurant hand in hand, Leah's entire body thrumming with excitement as he led her not back to their cars but onto the beach, which was bathed in moonlight and silent except for the gentle crashing of waves against the shore. She slipped off her heels and sank her toes into the sand, and he removed his blazer and draped it over her shoulders to shield her from the slight chill in the air.

Then they made their way down to the shoreline, his arm around her waist holding her close as the water lapped against their toes and the inky ocean spread out before them, shimmering into infinity. "Are you having a good time tonight?" he murmured above the sound of the sea, the lone cry of a seagull making its way back to shore.

"The best." Leah rested her head against his shoulder, breathing in his familiar scent of sandalwood. Then, in a playful tone, she said, "I had no idea you were such a gentleman. You really know how to treat a woman right."

He shrugged. "I wanted to make a good impression. Next time it's going to be canned spaghetti on paper plates in my backyard."

She laughed. "I can live with that." Then, tipping

her face up to his, she said, "You can kiss me, you know."

Ben went very still. "I wasn't sure if you'd want that. Or if you were ready for it."

She sighed. "I definitely want that. As for if I'm ready for it..." Her lips tipped up in a smile meant just for him. "There's only one way to find out."

He turned to her then, cupping her face in his hands, caressing her skin gently, reverently, as though one wrong touch and she would break. His breathing had quickened, matching hers, and she could feel the excitement, the trepidation, the wonder of all that had led them here enveloping them as the stars overhead stood sentinel to this moment when time went still.

"Leah..." Ben's breath was a whisper against her skin as he leaned toward her, his lips brushing hers for just a moment as a sigh escaped her.

And then her cell phone rang, shattering the silence and causing them both to jump apart, hearts pounding, expressions comically guilty, as if they had been doing something wrong.

"Sorry about that," Leah muttered, embarrassed but laughing as she reached into her purse to silence the call. But a moment later it started up again, the ring insistent, echoing against the cloudless sky.

When the phone fell silent and then immediately began ringing a third time, Leah felt the first pangs of worry in the pit of her stomach. "You should take it," Ben urged, catching sight of her expression. "It might be something important."

Leah's fears were confirmed when she checked the caller ID and saw Callie's name. Her daughter never called her three times in a row. Never.

"Hello?" she asked, fear creeping into her voice despite her best efforts. "Callie, is everything okay?"

"Mom?" Callie's voice was stained with tears. "It's Dad. There's been an accident."

CHAPTER 12

"Tell me you didn't do this. Tell me you didn't *do* this."

Max was pacing his room frantically, as he had been doing for the better part of the past twelve hours, wincing every time he passed the mirror and caught sight of his frazzled expression and wild hair. He had spent most of the day placing frenzied phone calls to the police department, trying to figure out where Vanessa was currently being housed.

Or perhaps he should say inmate number 7204 at MCC New York, otherwise known as federal prison.

Since locating her, he'd been trying desperately to get in touch, to hear her side of the story, but apparently placing calls to inmates was against the rules. He had to wait for her to contact him.

And so he waited. And waited. And waited some more, practically tearing his hair out, until his phone finally rang just as he was losing hope of getting some *answers*.

"Of course I didn't do it," she snapped, tone as biting as always. "What do you take me for?"

A woman obsessed with image. A woman who would rather die than give up her social status. A woman who would rob from sick children to accomplish that?

A woman he used to love.

"Well can you blame me for asking?" he shot back, anger pulsing through his veins once more as he tried to calculate just how much damage had already been done to him, both professionally and personally. Because he was no fool. Vanessa may not be guilty of everything she was charged with, but she was the subject of a federal investigation that landed her in prison pending a trial. What were the odds that they had made a mistake on all counts?

Slim to none.

"Of course I blame you for asking." Vanessa's voice had turned tearful now, though he wasn't moved in the least. "Max, I didn't do it. I didn't *do* it."

Max lowered himself onto the edge of the bed, massaging his temples, where a fierce headache was rapidly developing. "I suppose you're going to need a lawyer."

Vanessa didn't hesitate. "The best money can buy."

Max shook his head, unsure whether her words made him want to laugh or cry. When did she become so obsessed with money, and all the privileges that came with it? Or maybe she had always been that way, and he had been too blinded by her beauty and charm to realize it.

"Well... there's not much in the joint accounts, but take whatever you need," he conceded.

A very long pause, and then, "The joint accounts? Max, there's practically nothing in the joint accounts. It's dimes. *Pennies.* I need to dip into your account. It's the only way."

Max was already shaking his head, even though she couldn't possibly know that. "I'm sorry, Vanessa, that's not a possibility."

Indeed, they had agreed to keep some of their finances separate prior to their marriage, something Max was increasingly grateful for every day. Vanessa had undoubtedly drained her personal savings and their joint accounts, but Max's was still robust, thanks in part to the movie deal his first book had won long before he and Vanessa had met. His financial advisor at the time had recommended that he save the funds for future security, and he had taken the advice to heart.

"What?" Vanessa practically screeched. "You can't be serious, Max. I'm your *wife*. You *owe* me."

"We're separated," Max reminded her quietly. "And we both know that the only reason we're not divorced is because you didn't want your friends to find out. I'm fairly certain you used the words 'loser,' 'deadbeat,' and 'pathetic' to describe me on the day you demanded the separation."

Another long pause, followed by, "You're right, Max, I did say those things, but you have to understand that they were in the heat of the moment. I love you. I've always loved you. I've been wanting to call you, wanting to work things out, I just..."

"Didn't," he supplied. "Because you had no intentions of working things out. You don't love me, Vanessa, and I doubt very much you ever have. To you, I was always just a paycheck, until the money dried up. The *joint* money, that is."

"But Max," Vanessa wailed, "I'll have to get a public defender! Do you know what that means for me? Do you know what I'm facing? A decade, Max! A *decade*!"

"I'm sorry to hear that Vanessa," he said quietly. "I

hope for your sake that what they're saying you did isn't true. Because if it is, I don't know how you're going to live with yourself."

A shocked silence followed his declaration, and then, "You know what, Max? Everything I said about you is right. You are worthless. A washed-up loser with nothing to show for himself in the past ten years." Her voice was rising steadily, and her fury along with it. "You're going to regret this someday, Max. You're going to—"

But whatever he was going to do, Max would never know, because he hung up the phone and hurled it across the room, where it bounced off the bed and landed on the floor, face-down. Then, hearing laughter and conversation drifting in from the partially open window, he strode over to it and looked down at the beach below to find several dozen people milling around, drinks in hand, while tuxedo-clad waiters passed around trays of hors d'oeuvres and a string quartet played soft music in the background.

There was a party going on down there. And he had every intention of crashing it.

AVERY WAS HAVING trouble keeping her eyes off Danny, who looked more handsome than ever in a gray suit and indigo button-down that brought out the sparkle in his beautiful brown eyes. This was a problem, because she shouldn't be staring at the groom-to-be. Well, the *former* groom-to-be. Because after the kiss they'd shared, it was only a matter of time before he called off the wedding.

She felt a twinge of guilt every time Molly looked her way, then reminded herself that she had nothing to feel bad about. Danny was hers. He always had been. It had just taken a break and some perspective for him to realize that. They would handle the matter delicately, of course, because Avery was well aware the pain of a broken heart, and she had no ill will toward Molly.

She just wished Danny would look her way. She wished he would confirm that what had happened only a few short hours ago was real, and not just a desperate figment of her imagination.

But he had remained by Molly's side throughout the entire engagement party, holding her hand, tucking his arm around her waist, laughing at little things she said. Avery, keen to avoid seeing this at all costs, busied herself with ensuring that things ran smoothly, checking on the caterers, the bartender, the musicians, until there was nothing left for her to do but blend into the background, and make small talk with Danny's friends and family.

"This is some party."

Avery reeled around at the unexpected intrusion into her thoughts to find Max Wallace standing beside her. He looked awful—dark circles under his eyes, fatigue etched in every line of his face, his clothes rumpled and out of place for the elegant event. But she was glad to see him all the same, glad to have an ally, of sorts, as she watched the love of her life fawn over another woman.

Max nodded toward Danny, who was currently at the bar, grabbing drinks for himself and Molly. "Isn't that the guy you're after?"

Avery winced. When he put it that way, it sounded so... dirty.

Voice icy, she shot back, "I'm not 'after' anyone. Remember, he was mine first."

She realized how childish she sounded, and Max held up his hands to ward off her defensiveness. "Hey, I'm not judging. Remember, my wife is currently languishing in federal prison and my life is pretty much in the toilet." He slid a quick smile her way. "I was just clarifying the situation, that's all."

Avery made a noncommittal sound in the back of

her throat, her eyes still on Danny. Then, after several more moments of watching him cozy up to Molly, she said in a pained voice, "Why is he spending so much *time* with her? Believe it or not, they aren't actually joined at the hip."

Max's blue eyes had turned sympathetic. He, too, watched the couple for a time, then said, "I might be overstepping here, but... I think you're setting yourself up to get hurt."

"You don't know what you're talking about." Avery's tone wasn't curt, just matter-of-fact. Then, lowering her voice, she whispered, "Today, in the kitchen, he kissed me."

Max's eyebrows shot up into his hairline. "He kissed you? And now he's here at his engagement party with his fiancée." He shrugged. "Seems like a real prize, that one. But again." He pursed his lips. "Not my business."

"No, it's not." Suddenly, Avery was feeling mutinous. She glanced at her watch, hoping that time had sped up, but no. The party wasn't set to break up for another two hours.

Another two hours of complete torture.

"Avery, dear, I just wanted to commend you." Suddenly, Molly's mother Susan had appeared at Avery's side, precariously balancing a plate of hors d'oeuvres and a flute of champagne. "It's rare for divorced couples to get along so well, but the way you've welcomed Molly into your life has been nothing short of saint-like."

Susan hiccupped, and some of the champagne sloshed dangerously close to the rim. "But between you and me, I see the way you look at him." She wagged her finger in Avery's face. "Tsk tsk, dear. Don't worry, though, I won't say anything. My husband left me for another woman too, so I completely understand."

Another hiccup, and then she walked away, stumbling slightly, without another word.

"Well, that was awkward," Max said into the silence as Avery's cheeks burned with embarrassment. "But hey, look on the bright side—she's probably not going to remember any of that in the morning." He took Avery gently by the arm and led her toward the bar. "Come on, let's get you a drink. I have a feeling you're going to need one."

"So how are things with you?" Avery asked as they took their places in line. "Did you have a chance to speak with Vanessa?"

"Oh, we spoke all right." Max's shoulders stiffened. "I think we probably won't have too much contact for a while." He turned to Avery with a guilty expression. "I'm sorry again about all the commotion this morning. I hope it doesn't happen again."

"If it does, we'll deal with it," Avery said with a shrug. "Really, it wasn't a big deal. Okay, it *was* a big deal," she consented, smiling as he shot her a dubious look. "But it wasn't your fault. I know you came to Crystal Bay for peace and quiet, and I hope this doesn't put a wrench in that plan." She grinned at him. "Do you still like our little slice of heaven?"

"Like it? I'm obsessed with it." Max gestured out toward the navy blue water churning gently in the background. "Who wouldn't be? You're lucky to call a place like this home. I can't imagine returning to Manhattan after waking up to this every day. It seems... unthinkable."

"Then stay." The two of them approached the bartender and gave their orders—scotch on the rocks for him, a green apple martini for her. "You're an author, right? That means you can write from pretty much anywhere. Besides," she added with a wink, "I won't say no to you booking a room at the inn for an extra couple of months. A girl's gotta eat, you know."

He laughed. "You help me sell my next book, and we'll talk."

Just then, a clinking sound drew their attention

toward a table at the front of the party, where Danny and Molly had stood from their chairs and were smiling at their assembled guests, hand in hand. Avery felt yet another swoop of nausea at the sight of them together, but she did her best to feign a smile—and interest in whatever they were about to say.

"Thank you, everyone, for coming tonight," Danny said as the crowd quieted and everyone turned to listen. "It means so much to us"—he tucked Molly closer to his side—"that we have your love and support as we enter this next phase of our lives. And I couldn't be more excited for what the future holds with this woman beside me."

He turned and gazed deeply into Molly's eyes, and she raised her hand and caressed her fingers down his cheek. Beside Avery, Max shifted uncomfortably, and she could feel his eyes like twin brands on her skin.

"And with that in mind"—Danny took a deep breath—"we wanted to make a little announcement, and since so many of the people we love are here tonight, we thought this would be the most appropriate time to do it."

He gave Molly one last adoring smile, the same one he used to turn on Avery, and said, "Our little family of two is soon going to be adding one more."

As the crowd let out a collective gasp of excitement, he concluded, grinning, "In a few months, I'm going to be a father, and this woman beside me is going to be the most amazing mother I could ever imagine. That's right, folks... we're expecting!"

A round of enthusiastic clapping followed, and then the guests began swarming toward the couple, everyone eager to congratulate them on their news.

Everyone except Avery, that is. She was too busy collapsing against Max as her world crashed down around her and the future she had once more dared to believe in turned to ashes at her feet.

CHAPTER 13

"**M**om! Oh, thank goodness you're here."

Callie's eyes were red-rimmed and her face was splotchy as Leah folded her daughter into her arms. Behind them, Andrew was pacing the hospital waiting room, his hair standing in all directions from what must have been hours of running his fingers through it. The sharp tang of antiseptic permeated the air around them, and the steady hum of beeps from the patients' rooms formed a drumbeat to their collective fear.

Leah had hopped in her car as soon as she'd gotten the call and headed directly for the city, her mind racing with the worst kinds of images, her heart in her throat, a ball of terror in her stomach.

She and Phil may have been in a dark place right now, but he was still her husband. He was still the man she had shared nearly three decades of her life with. He was still her children's father, and her future grandchildren's grandpa. If something happened to him, she would be devastated.

Amid Callie's sobbing over the phone, she'd managed to work out that Phil had been on a job site, inspecting the roof on a new building, when he had slipped and fallen. In addition to broken bones, he had sustained a head injury, and doctors also feared internal bleeding. Right now, it was touch and go, and her children were terrified they were going to lose their father, who, despite what he had done to Leah, had always been a stable, loving presence in their lives.

"How is he?" Leah released her daughter and brushed her tear-soaked hair back from her face. "Any updates? Can I see him?"

"No updates," Andrew chimed in, ashen-faced, as Callie shook her head. "He hasn't regained consciousness since the fall. And he's only allowed one visitor in his room at a time right now."

"I'm going to check on him then, see if I can track down a doctor and get some answers." Leah made to walk out of the waiting room, but Callie stopped her with a hand on her arm.

"Kate's in there with him right now," she said. "I called her when I found out what happened. I thought she would want to know, since the three of you have always been so close…" She trailed off uncertainly at the sight of Leah's frozen expression. "That's okay, right? I figured we could all use some extra support right now…" Her voice died off again as she glanced at Andrew, who was watching Leah carefully.

"Of course." Leah cleared her throat and squeezed her daughter's hand. "Of course it's okay. I'll give them another minute or two, and then I'll pop into his room and check on him."

"Come on, I'll show you where it is."

Callie dabbed her eyes dry with the tissue balled in her fist and beckoned for Leah to follow her out of the waiting room. She drew her arms around herself protectively as they strode down the sterile hallway, trying not to get in the way of the nurses and doctors bustling past them. "It's just down the hall on the right," Callie said as they bypassed a man on a stretcher. When they reached Phil's door, she stuck her head inside while Leah caught up to her—

And they both looked into the room at the same

time a silently weeping Kate, whose back was to them, smoothed the hair on a motionless Phil's head before bending down to kiss him on the lips.

CALLIE WAS TREMBLING with shock as Leah escorted her back into the waiting room, her own mind racing as she tried to come to terms with what she had just seen.

Her friends were right. The rumors were true. Phil and Kate were... an item?

Andrew, face pale, looked as though he was about to pass out when he caught sight of Callie's expression. "Is it Dad? Is he—?"

"No, no, your father's fine," Leah immediately interjected. Then, backpedaling, she corrected, "Well, not *fine*, but he's the same, as far as we could tell." She glanced at Callie, who was now slumped in one of the waiting room chairs, head in her hands. "We walked in on Kate..."

"Kissing him." Callie filled in the void when Leah hesitated. "She was *kissing* him. On the lips." Her eyes were haunted when they met Leah's. "This is why you left. Because the two of them..." She pressed her hands to her mouth in disgust. "I think I'm going to be sick."

Leah sat down beside her daughter, then motioned for Andrew to do the same. When the three of them were seated, she took each of her children's hands in her own and, seeing the pain in their eyes, shook her head and said softly, "I don't want you to hate your father over this. You can hate what he's done, but he's always been good to you, and I know how much you love him. Let's not have this tear our family apart any more than it already has." She gave each of their hands a gentle squeeze. "Okay?"

"How can you be so calm about this?" Callie said, shooting her mother a look of disbelief. "How can you be *okay* with this?"

"I'm not 'okay' with this, and I never will be." Leah turned to gaze out the window at the midnight sky, and imagined, for just a moment, that she was standing on the edge of paradise, her toes in the sand, the warm water lapping against her ankles... and her hand safely entwined with someone else's.

Then she turned to her children, eyes shining with tears of sadness for what had been, and happiness for what was to come. "But I'm fine. Believe me, I'm going to be fine."

~

"MOLLY, can I talk to you for a few minutes?"

Avery felt lightheaded as she approached Molly, who was sitting in the parlor at the inn, waiting for Danny to finish work for the day. She had a hand on her stomach, stroking it lovingly, and if Avery looked close enough—which she was trying very hard not to do—she could see the first hints of a baby bump.

"Of course." Molly gave her a genuine smile and gestured to the seat beside her, and Avery lowered herself into it, exhaling a deep, calming breath as she crossed one leg over the other and forced herself to meet Molly's eyes.

"There's something I need to tell you. Something I need to apologize for." Avery gazed down at her hands, clenching and unclenching her fists, working up the courage to release the words that needed to be said. The ones that had needed to be said from the start.

"Okay…" Molly's tone was hesitant as she turned in her seat to face Avery, her eyes warm with concern. It struck Avery then that in a different time, in a different life… the two of them could have been friends. "Is everything okay?"

"No. It's not." Avery swallowed hard, felt the tears beginning to build, but this time, she didn't try to hide them. This time, she let them fall. She felt Molly slip her hand into hers, a gesture of comfort that only made the tears fall faster. She didn't deserve this woman's sympathy. Not after what she had done.

She glanced up and met Molly's eyes once more, steeling herself, then said, "I'm sorry for whatever trouble this is going to cause you, but Molly... you and Danny can't get married at the inn." She brushed away some of the falling tears as Molly's eyes widened in shock. "It's killing me," she confessed. "And this inn is my home. It's my heart and soul, and... I can't let it be the place where Danny officially moves on. He and I have too much shared history. I was too devastated after we divorced, and that's not your fault. You've been lovely, but I just... can't."

Molly was silent for several long moments after that, her eyes sweeping over Avery's face while the latter held her breath, fearful of the response. Then, to her immense relief, Molly gave her a small smile and squeezed her hand softly. "It's okay, Avery. I understand. I just wish you would have said something sooner, saved yourself a lot of heartache."

She shook her head. "I did question Danny's decision to have the wedding here, but he was adamant that you would be fine with it. In hindsight, I can see I should have insisted we have it somewhere else. I hope you can forgive me for that."

She squeezed Avery's hand again. "I was married once before too, you know. I thought it was going to be forever, that he was the love of my life. Unfortunately, the two of us haven't managed to get along quite as well as you and Danny—we can't be in the same room as each other. Or I should say that I can't be in the same room as him and his new wife. It brings up too many painful memories for me." She sighed. "So sadly, I know where you're coming from. And I'm more than happy to find another place for our wedding. Just… next time, talk to me, okay? I don't want you to view me as the enemy."

"Thank you." Somehow, Molly's show of support only made Avery feel worse. Then, wiping a fresh wave of tears from her eyes, she whispered once more, "I'm sorry." Though this time, she was apologizing for something else.

"Oh, honey, you have nothing to be sorry for." Molly shot her another smile and then released her hand. "Danny and I just want you to be happy."

"I will be." Avery took another deep breath,

preparing herself for yet another difficult conversation to come. "Soon, I will be."

"WE NEED TO TALK."

An hour later, an exhausted and slightly nauseated Molly gave up waiting for Danny to finish his work for the evening and had gone home, but not before folding Avery into a long hug that brought tears to her eyes and another twist of guilt to her chest. Since their conversation, Avery had been poring over every word Molly said, and she'd decided that Danny's fiancée was right.

Molly wasn't the enemy, and never had been.

Danny glanced up from the desk, where he had been tallying up credit card receipts on the computer, as Avery approached. "What's up?"

Avery could feel her fury building at his nonchalant tone but tried her best to tamp down on it. In the darkest hours of the night following Danny's announcement at the engagement party, she'd decided not to confront him about what had happened between the two of them. There was no point—the blinders had been lifted, and she now saw him for what he was. She now saw him for who he had always been.

A selfish man. One who had tossed her away like yesterday's trash, then strung her along for years until tossing her away once more.

And she had let him. Well, no more of *that*.

"Danny." She inhaled sharply, trying to calm her nerves. He gave her a curious look, no hint of fear in his eyes. He wasn't worried in the least that she would tell Molly about the kiss—another sign of his arrogance that she had missed. Or overlooked, because she loved him.

Banishing the memory of his lips on hers, and the price she had paid for allowing him into her heart once more, she pressed on, hands clenched so tight her knuckles were slowly bleeding to white. "I don't want to be partners anymore. I want you to leave the inn."

If she had expected Danny to be shocked, or angry, or to show any emotion whatsoever, she would have been sorely disappointed. He wasn't invested in the inn. It didn't mean to him what it did to Avery—for him, it was just another job.

Just like she had been just another woman, easily replaceable. Their life together hadn't meant to him what it had meant to Avery. At least now she knew the truth, and could finally begin to pick up the pieces and move on.

Danny leaned back in his chair, scratching his chin thoughtfully, and said, "You know, I think that's probably a good idea." He swept his arm around the foyer. "This place was always your dream, not mine, and lately I've been itching to do something else with my life." He sighed. "But there's a problem. I know you don't have the money to buy me out, and I can't afford to just walk away."

Avery nodded. "I know. And I'll figure it out, somehow."

"Okey-dokey. Once you have a plan, let me know, and we'll talk." Danny returned his attention to the computer, as if their conversation had been about something as mundane as the weather, and not the final severing of the life they had shared for twenty years.

Avery stood there, staring at him, a single tear tracking down her cheek as she said a silent goodbye to the man who had held her heart in the palm of his hand since she was just a girl, the man who had promised her the moon and stars and then taken it all away without a second thought.

Yes, this was a goodbye. But it was also a hello. To herself, for a change.

"Okey-dokey," she whispered beneath her breath, and then, shoulders held high, she pushed open the screen door and stepped out onto the porch, where she was surprised to find Max sitting in an Adirondack chair and gazing out at the cerulean sea, his computer lying forgotten in his lap.

"I suppose you heard all of that," she said, easing herself into the chair beside him with a long, tired sigh.

"I wasn't trying to." He shot her an apologetic look. "But I'm glad I did."

Avery cocked her head at him. "And why is that?"

"Because I have someone who would make the perfect partner for you. Someone who can buy out your ex-husband's half of the inn right now. He doesn't know a whole lot about running an inn, but he's a quick learner, and a hard worker, and recently… he's been looking for a big change in his life. And he thinks this might be just the thing he needs."

At this, Avery's ears perked up, and a cautious optimism settled over her. "Oh? And who might this be?"

Max smiled at her, and in that moment, the rest of the world melted away, leaving her with tendrils of something that felt a lot like hope—*real* hope—unfurling in her chest like butterflies.

"Me."

LEAH RETURNED to Crystal Bay early the next day, having stayed with her children at the hospital long into the night. Phil had woken in the wee hours of the morning, and fortunately, the doctors' fears of internal bleeding had turned out to be unfounded. Leah didn't linger by his bedside, just wished him the best before saying goodbye to Andrew and Callie —and squeezing her daughter extra tight—before making the drive home.

She hadn't seen Kate. Nor did she want to. That was her past now, and this... this was her present.

Ben answered the door looking adorably rumpled, like he had just rolled out of bed, and when he saw her standing on his porch, he immediately perked up. "Leah! What are you doing here? How's—"

But he never had the chance to finish that sentence. His eyes widened in surprise and delight as Leah stepped forward and folded herself into his arms, breathing in his familiar scent and allowing the memories of years long past to wash over her. Memories of a girl in love with a boy, though she never had the courage to tell him.

That time had finally come, though she had no intention of saying it with words.

Instead, she stood on tiptoe and cupped his face in her hands, and the kiss that followed was long, and slow, and leisurely, an oh-so-gentle exploration of each other's lips, an admission of all that they meant to each other and a promise that this, right here, right now, was only the beginning.

EPILOGUE

hen she heard the knock, Cynthia Hart immediately slid the paper she had been writing on beneath a stack of books, then dabbed the tears from her eyes and checked her makeup in the mirror before crossing her small apartment to open the door. Her oldest daughter was standing on the threshold, looking defiant, but also something else.

Happy. Luminously happy.

"Leah! What a surprise." Cynthia opened the door wider to allow her to step inside. "Come on in. Would you like a slice of cheesecake?"

"No thanks. I can't stay for long." Leah took a deep breath, then said, "I just wanted you to know that I've officially filed for divorce from Phil. And I won't hear another word to the contrary from you. Have I made myself clear?"

Cynthia smiled to herself, though her face betrayed no emotion. Her oldest daughter was feisty, like her father, a realization that brought with it a profound sense of sadness for all she had lost. For all Leah had lost, too.

"Crystal clear." Cynthia beckoned her daughter inside, and this time, she reluctantly followed her through the apartment to the pair of chairs Cynthia kept by the window. The apartment wasn't much to write home about, but it had breathtaking ocean views, and a deck just big enough to fit a table for one, perfect for enjoying her morning tea with the sun and sea.

Lowering herself into one of the chairs, Cynthia gazed at her daughter intently. "Are you happy, then? This is what you want?"

"It is, and I am." Some of the tension bled from Leah's shoulders, and she could see her daughter visibly relaxing. Then, "But why did you fight so hard for Phil, Mom? Especially after everything he did? I can't understand it."

The questions were valid. They also nearly broke her.

"I just wanted you to make the right decision,

dear," she said in a deliberately vague tone. "Breaking up a marriage isn't something to be taken lightly." She sounded like a broken record, and she knew it—but she wasn't ready for her daughters to know the truth. Not yet.

Leah was quiet for several moments after that, watching the waves rolling gently to shore, and then, with a curt nod, she said, "Well, I did make the right decision. And I'd like your support." Standing, she headed for the door. "I'll see you later, okay? I have a few errands to run. Anything I can grab for you?"

"No, I'm fine. But thank you." Cynthia ushered her daughter out the door, then closed it softly behind her, leaning her head against the smooth wood and releasing a long sigh. These past few weeks had been among the hardest of her life, and she knew that the battle she was facing would be long, and difficult, and heartbreaking… for her, and for her daughters.

With that in mind, she returned to the stack of books, moving them aside to reveal the paper beneath. Then, lifting her pen once more, she stared at the lines of notes she'd made under a simple title:

Cynthia's Last Hurrah

She stared at the page then, tears forming in her

eyes, rereading all the things she had yet to do in a life that now seemed far too short.

Something was missing.

She knew what it was, of course. But did she have the courage to write it down? And moreover, did she have the courage to actually go *through* with it?

Only time would tell. But the list would forever be incomplete without it.

And so, with a wistful smile on her lips, she wrote the five simple words that she knew might change everything.

See Edward one last time.

THE STORY CONTINUES in book three, **Secrets at Crystal Bay**. Click here to grab your copy!

Get a free book! To instantly receive *The Inn at Dolphin Bay*, the first novel in my most popular series, join my Reader Club at www. miakent.com/dolphin.

Thank you so much for your support!

Love,

Mia

ABOUT THE AUTHOR

Mia Kent is the author of clean, contemporary women's fiction and small-town romance. She writes heartfelt stories about love, friendship, happily ever after, and the importance of staying true to yourself.

She's been married for over a decade to her high school sweetheart, and when she isn't working on her next book, she's chasing around a toddler, crawling after an infant, and hiding from an eighty-pound tornado of dog love. Frankly, it's a wonder she writes at all.

To learn more about Mia's books, to sign up for her email list, or to send her a message, visit her website at www.miakent.com.

Made in United States
North Haven, CT
25 February 2024

49140759R00136